12 DAYS OF C

BY

FRED LEIGH.

First published by Rose Bank Publishing 1996.
Copyright Fred Leigh
All rights reserved

ISBN 0 9524198 3 1

No part of this publication may be reproduced, Stored in a retrieval system or transmitted in any form or by any means, electronic, mechanical, photocopying, recording or otherwise, without the prior permission of the publisher and author.

Type setting and design by
Rose Bank Publishing
11 Church Lane,
Oulton,
Stone,
Staffs.
ST15 8UL.
Tel: 01785 813633

By the same author.

Sentinel Street
Potteries at War
Tales of Old Hanley
Mining Memories
St. John the Evangelist Oulton
(Notu Dignum)
Most Valiant of Men
Lest We Forget
Sentinel Street (2nd Edition)
North Staffs Dialect

PLAYS

The Soldier's Return
The Conversion
A Place in the Country

THE SENTINEL

Christmas Stories
Articles

B.B.C. RADIO STOKE.

(Tapes and Recordings)
Tales of Old Hanley
The Most Valiant of Men
Sentinel Street

Foreword

The popular Christmas carol which provides the title for this collection of stories, celebrates the giving of lavish gifts to loved ones over the festive period.

Most of the North Staffordshire characters in Fred Leigh's tales would have welcomed having a pear to tuck into on Christmas Day, let alone the partridge sitting in the tree.

Yet for all the poverty and hardship endured by these struggling families, their humour and generosity shines through in this heart warming collection of stories, all steeped in local dialect and history.

As a former miner myself, and someone whose family have worked in the industry for generations, it is particularly pleasing that the characters, the camaraderie and the conditions of the pits are recalled so vividly.

It is essential that generations to come are able to read about the human history behind the traditional industries on which North Stafford's heritage is founded.

Above all, however, this book helps to remind us that the real spirit of Christmas is often found in humour, and generosity of families unable to lavish money on expensive presents.

Season's Greetings,

Councillor George O'Kane Cairns,
Mayor of Newcastle, 1996-97.

Preface

Some of these stories have been published before. Some have been published by The Sentinel as long ago as 1985, and about two in my previous books, but nevertheless there are many people who have not, may I be permitted to say , had the pleasure. So I deemed that for a few not forgotten tales of Christmas ought to be in one book.

They are stories of a bygone age from the late 19th century to the second world war, portraying what life was like in that era, a bit of nostalgia and perhaps a study of social history. Some are grim, some are full of humour, and typical of the people of the area that I write about.

Twelve days of Christmas,
My true love gave to me.

Acknowledgments

Councillor G. O'Kane Cairns Mayor of Newcastle, Foreword.
Ron Leigh, Publishing
John Abberley, The Sentinel.
Steve Rodgers, Illustrations.
Mrs. M.W. White, for the use of paintings by her late husband
Ernest H. White.
The Hot Potato Machine, Holy Trinity Church, Hanley Market Square, Electric Theatre, The Lyric Cinema, Albion Square, Waggon and Horses.
Pauline Shufflebotham for the Ode
" A pub crawl in days of old"
Freda Martin, Oulton.

Contents

	CHAPTER	PAGE
1	The Soldier's Bible.	1
2	The Good Samaritans	9
3	The One Pound Note.	17
4	Yanks for the Memory.	25
5	A Christmas Hot Pot	31
6	Spirits of Retribution	45
7	Christmas Day in the Workhouse.	53
8	A Prayer for Christmas.	59
9	The Conversion.	65
10	The Pub Crawl	75
11	The Healing.	83
12	He That Is Without Sin.	88

Chapter 1
THE SOLDIER'S BIBLE.

John was in a state of deep depression. For a week ago his company, where he had laboured for many years, had gone into liquidation, and he was now unemployed. He had not told his wife Mary, and had left home the same time in the mornings and returned in the evening as usual. How could he thought, care and provide for her and his two children, Jimmy and little Alice. Christmas was nigh and there would be nothing for any of them. He had tried everywhere to find employment but to no avail.

His mind was in a turmoil, he felt that he had failed them and he had decided to end it all. He had made provision for them and in his present state of mind they would be better off without him. On his way to the pre-determined place, the canal at Etruria to shake off his mortal coil, he was about to pass the Holy Trinity Church in Trinity Street he espied, on the notice board:-

Book Sale in the Church Hall,
in aid of Church Funds.

John was an avid reader, and subconsciously made his way there. An elderly man with snow white hair and beard sat at one of the stalls who watched John as he picked up and replaced several books. He was about to leave when his interest was aroused by a much worn book bound in black linen. The title in faded gold letters read:- 'The Soldiers Bible.'

Taking up the book he noticed that on the closed pages written in bold black figures the number, 5044756. This he thought would be the soldier's number. On the back of the front cover was written:-

Corporal William Henshall,
5th. Battalion North
Staffs Regiment.
Served in Sudan, India, France 1914-

Holy Trinity Church
Trinity Street Hanley

The elderly man at the stall eyed John intently as he turned the pages of the bible. In the book of Matthew, chapter 7 verse 7: was underlined in red ink, it read:-Ask and it shall be given you; seek, and ye shall find.

Again in Matthew, chapter 16, verse 26: For what is a man profited, if he shall gain the whole world, and lose his own soul. Or what shall a man give in exchange for his soul? Strange he thought. Why should a soldier note these two verses, philosophical they may be. But why? A piece of folded paper that seemed to act as a book mark for the page. He opened it slowly to reveal in neat writing:-

Somewhere in France December 24th. 1916.
My Dearest Wife Mary......

This was a letter to the mans wife, meant for her only he thought and folded it then closed the bible. He was about to return the bible to the others on the stall, when the elderly man with white hair and beard put his hand on John's arm.

''*Take the bible my son,*'' he said softly.

''*I,I can't, I can't afford it.*'' John replied rather embarrassed.

''*Please, I insist. Accept it as gift from me.*'' A smile appeared on the elderly mans face. ''*I can see that you are deeply troubled my son, take it. It will help you I'm sure. I ask only that you do something for me.*''

''*What is that?*'' asked John.

''*Go from here and enter the church. Open the bible and read again what Matthew wrote. Think deeply about the meaning then read the letter.*''

''*I couldn't read the letter. Surely a mans thoughts to his wife are private, sacrosanct.*''

''*So they are my son. But in it you will find hope and comfort. You see I knew the soldier, he was a good man a comrade. He was killed two days later in the carnage that was to follow. If it is to serve a purpose, I am sure that now is the time. Please take it, read the letter*

"Take the bible my son,"

and may the Lord be with you."

"I,I er don't know what to say," John said quietly with emotion as he looked into the eyes of the elderly man with the white hair and beard. *"Thank you,"* he uttered at last.

With the bible clutched in his hand, he turned and walked from the building. He entered the church, the silence and sanctity overawed him, he felt somehow that a presence was watching him. In the nearest pew he knelt and started to pray. He remained deep in prayer for some time with the bible held in his hands. Then, his shoulders heaved and he started to sob. At last he arose from his knees and sat down, taking an handkerchief from his pocket wiped the tears from his eyes. Opening the bible he took out the letter and read:

> *My Dearest Wife Mary, It is Christmas Eve again sweetheart, how I miss you and my children. I long with all my heart to be with you in our little house, warm and safe to celebrate the birth of Christ, in our humble way to give thanks for what little we have and pray for peace for all mankind. It is quiet here now my love, the noise of war silent for a little while. A flurry of snow is falling, but the sky is clear and the stars shine brightly. From across the war ravaged land a strange yet wonderful sound fills the winter sky, "Stille Nacht, Heilige Nacht", then a boyish voice near to me in our muddy trench joined in singing, "Silent Night, Holy Night, then another until a full choir all in unison 'till the end. Oh so beautiful Mary. For that short space in time it seemed that we were in a great cathedral, our troubles and discomfort were forgotten because of Christmas. Why Mary do we go on to kill one another? Life is so precious, we have so much to live for however hard and unbearable it sometime seems. Christmas is over and it starts all over again......*

The letter ended there and John realised that before the soldier had time to finish the letter, just after the Christmas lull the blood letting had resumed and he was killed. John left the church, he felt better now and was deep in thought about the bible and the letter. His troubles seemed petty compared with those that suffered and were sacrificed in that terrible war. He was alive and healthy, a good wife and family. He shuddered when he thought of his previous intention.

Walking slowly up Trinity Street, just outside the Evening Sentinel building, he saw a wallet on the ground. He picked it up and opened it and found that it contained a considerable sum of money.

More money than he could earn in several months when he was in work. What a find, he thought, his troubles were now definitely over. He'd buy a goose or even a turkey, a nice present for his wife and toys for the children. His joy at finding the wallet knew no bounds. Gripping the bible in one hand and the wallet in the other, he smiled, "Seek and ye shall find", the good book stated a good omen he thought, and was about to put the wallet into his pocket when the other verse flashed in his mind. "For what is a man profited, if he shall gain the whole world and lose his own soul?" The smile vanished from his face. 'What is happening to me, what does it all mean?' The voices within his head continued, 'Go on take it, enjoy it'. Another urged, 'Return to him to whom it belongs. Remember what Matthew wrote in the bible. 'Knock and it shall be opened unto you'. John opened the wallet and found a business card. On it was printed:-

Charles Turner,
Managing Director,
Turner Engineering,

with an address in Hanley. Without further ado he made his way there. He paused at the office door, the temptation of keeping the wallet returned, he was about to turn away and give in, when the image of the elderly man with the white hair and beard entered is mind. "Knock, and it will be opened unto you", the image said. "Remember Matthew, the bible". He knocked at the door, the door was opened by a young woman who asked his business.

"*I've found a wallet and I believe it belongs to a Mr. Turner.*" John said.

"*Oh,*" she replied. "*Please wait here I am sure Mr. Turner would like to see you*".

She walked to an inner office door, knocked and entered. In a few moments she re-appeared holding the door ajar.

"*Would you please come this way,*" she said smiling.

Mr. Turner with hand outstretched shook him by the hand and offered him a chair.

"*I believe you have found my wallet,*" he said smiling.

''Yes sir,'' John replied handing it to him.

Mr. Turner took it from him, his eyes never leaving the man sitting in front of him.

''I am very grateful to you. You must allow me to reward you for your honesty.''

He opened the wallet and withdrew several white five pound notes and offered them to John.

''Thank you sir, it is very generous of you, but I must decline your offer.''

''You amaze me,'' said Mr. Turner. *''Surely it must have been a great temptation to keep all the contents of the wallet, times are hard and Christmas near, and now you refuse my offer of a reward. Why?''*

''I must admit sir, I was greatly tempted, you see I am unemployed with a wife and two children.''

''What may I ask is your trade or calling?'' asked Mr. Turner.

''I am a time served engineer sir. The company I worked for closed a few weeks ago, and I am unable to find employment.''

''How strange,'' said an amazed Mr. Turner smiling.

''Very strange indeed. You see, this very morning I went to the Sentinel Office to place an advert for a man with your qualifications to fill a vacancy in my company, that is where I must have mislaid my wallet. I would like to offer you that position.''

Of course John accepted. He was overjoyed and ran with all speed to the church hall to tell the elderly man with the white hair and beard the good news. He approached the stall, he was disappointed the old man was nowhere to be seen. Sitting at the stall was a much younger man.

''Could you tell me where the elderly man with the white hair and beard is?'' John asked. *''He was in attendance here earlier today.''*

''An elderly man with white hair and beard, here at this stall?''

''Yes,'' said John *''This was the stall of that I am sure. He sat where you are sitting earlier today. Surely, he must have been here,*

I was talking to him and he gave me this bible."

The man shook his head and looked at John strangely .
"*I tell you he couldn't have been, I've been here all day and only left for a few minutes to fetch a cup of tea and a sandwich."*

On Christmas Eve John returned to the Holy Trinity Church in Trinity street for Midnight Mass. He went to give thanks and hoped with all his heart that he would meet again the elderly man with the white hair and beard. Sadly he did not, and he remains an enigma. John thrived in his job and was soon promoted. The bible, that was given pride of place in his book case. Every Christmas it is placed with reverence beneath the tree, and John emotions stirred, says a prayer and thinks of the elderly man with the white hair and beard.

Chapter 2
THE GOOD SAMARITANS.

A long time ago in 1926 A.D. This great nation of ours came to a standstill, and some 4,000,000 came out of work in sympathy with the miners', and a revolution began. Alas, after nine days the revolt ended, no shot had been fired and no one had been killed. The miners' however, were left to battle alone for seven long months of deprivation and despair.

Never before had there been such a desperate struggle, and finally a few weeks before Christmas, they lost the battle. A battle that they and their families, had fought and suffered so bravely. They had to accept lower wages and work longer hours. For some, there was no job to return to, because they had been blacklisted by the owners, and some pits had been allowed to flood and would never produce coal again. Jack Stevenson was one of these men.

Jack and his wife Mary, had four children their ages ranging from six to fifteen. Jack sat in the humble living room of his house, which was almost bereft of furniture, with his head cradled in his hands.

"*Ah dunna know wot wey're gooin'ter do Mary?*" he moaned.

"*Well wot did thee say at pit this mornin?*" Mary asked.

"*Pit! Thee inna any pit no more.*" Jack replied lifting his head to answer her. "*The buggers', the owners, 'ave let it flood anna thee.*"

"*But wey, strikes o'er inna it?*" Mary queried.

"*Oh ah strikes o'er. Wot good it's done us. It's there wey ah serpose, ter sey bugger yer. Yer've managed o' this tarme wi' ite it, na see 'ow yer con manage when it inna theer any moor*".

"*But anna thee cuttin' off their nose ter spite their face? It dunna make sense ter mey.*" Mary expounded.

"*It dunna matter ter them woman. They con afode it. They've 'ad their pennorth ite of it. Thee dunna give a sod abite us do thee?*"

Jack replied with bitterness in his voice.

"Wot's ter become of us Jack? Wot about the kids, an' Christmas coming on?" Mary asked and, bringing her pinafore to her face started to sob.

"Ah dunna no Mary lass. Ah just dunna know"

Jack and Mary's eldest daughter, Ethel, was 15 years old and on leaving school, went into service as a scullery maid with a well to do family near Stafford. Ethel, during one of her days holiday had taken her youngest brother Ken, to see the big house where she worked. On that particular day, the Womens' Institute were holding a meeting with the lady of the house.

When the meeting was over, the women departed to their own homes to the nearby village. Ethel was showing young Ken the gardens when one of the women stopped and spoke to them.

"Good afternoon Ethel, and who may I ask, is this young gentleman with you?"

"Good afternoon Missus Wilson. This is my youngest brother Kenneth. I've brought him to see the house and the garden. I thought a few hours in the country would do him good."

"So it will my dear I am sure," And so saying, held out her hand to young Ken. *"I am very pleased to meet you young man."* In all his six years Ken had never met such a lady and was rather taken back at being spoken to like that, and being offered a hand in the bargain. He was shy and at a loss how to answer.

"Well lad have yer lost yer tongue?" asked Ethel poking Ken in the side. *" Say Hello and please ter meet you Missus Wilson."*

*"Ppleased ter meet yer missus," h*e replied shyly, looking up at her and then letting his gaze fall quickly to examine his black plimsolls.

"I'm afraid 'e's a bit shy Missus Wilson."

"How are things at home now Ethel, now that the strike is over?"

"Things are very bad ma'am. Dad's pit is flooded and 'e's still not working. I don't know 'ow they're goin' ter manage, they only get

a bit of relief you see, and there's Christmas comin'. Me mam's at 'er wits end.''

''I am sorry my dear. How many are at home now?'' asked Mrs. Wilson.

''There's me mam and dad, 'im 'ere and, me young sister and brother,'' replied Ethel.

''Tut tut.'' Mrs. Wilson remarked. *''Quite a lot of mouths to feed. You of course live in here, don't you''?*

''Yes Ma'am.''

Mrs. Wilson stood deep in thought for a few moments looking intently at young Ken.

She took a small note pad and pencil from her hand bag.

''I am going to see if I can do something for your family, I am not going to promise anything now but I will try. Will you give me your parents name and address?''

A few days later a letter arrived at the Stevenson's. Jack opened it eagerly, and with some anticipation, for it was a rare occurrence for the Stevenson household to receive mail.

''Well wot does it see?'' asked an impatient Mary.

''It's from a Missus Wilson, 'er knows ah Ethel and it seems 'ers took a fancy to young Ken, an' would lark nowt better than 'ave ah young 'un fer Christmas.''

He passed the letter to Mary.

'' 'Ere yo read it an tell us wot yo think.''

''Well,'' said Mary after reading the letter,

'' 'Er seems genuine enough and as 'er says 'ers got no kids of 'er own an' 'er would bey pleased ter 'ave 'im.''

''Well, wot d'yer think?'' Jack asked.

''Ee ah dunner no. Ah'd miss the lad. In any case would 'e goo?''

'' 'Ed be a young foo' if 'e did'na. Thee'll bey nowt 'ere for 'im.''

When young Ken came from school, Jack and Mary told him of the contents of the letter.

"Me?" he asked in surprise, *"Why me?"*

" 'Ers took a fancy to thee lad that's wey," said Jack. *"It's an offer they cos'na refuse lad. Just think on it. Livin' in a posh 'ouse wi' thee own toys, better than 'ere cos ah conna give they or any on yer owt fer Christmas. Thee knows't that dust na?"*

Jack spoke the last few words with a tremor in his voice, his head bowed and his hands clenched showing the white in his knuckles. Silence ensued for several moments and, young Ken realising his father's anguish, put his hand on his shoulder.

"It's alright dad, ah'll goo if yer want me to."

Jack looked at his young son and smiled.

"Good lad. It wunna bey fer long, and just think they't see just 'ow the other 'aif live, a bit different than this poverty stricken place ah can tell thee lad."

A week before Christmas, on Ethel's day off, young Ken made his departure hand in hand with his sister. They turned to wave good bye to their parents when they reached the corner of the street. Jack and Mary were standing on the doorstep waving in return.

They turned to wave good bye

It was a large house in its own grounds. Ethel with Ken in tow, walked up the gravel drive to the front door and rang the bell. The door opened revealing a beaming Mrs. Wilson.

"Welcome to my house Kenneth. I am so very pleased that you accepted my invitation. Do please come in."

They entered the hall which seemed, to young Ken, larger than the whole of his parents house. He stared in amazement at the fine furniture and the large staircase. Young Ken was shown a bedroom that was to be his own, and was left alone to unpack his meagre clothing which he had brought in a brown paper parcel. How fine everything looked to him who had shared a bedroom with three others, all in the same bed. The silence of the room was eerie except for the rustle of the trees outside and the bird song. How different he thought, to the environment he had been brought up in. But a feeling of loneliness seemed to tug at his heart and he felt terribly depressed to the point of crying. Mr. Wilson was a good humoured sort of man, balding and with a fresh complexion, who took to Ken right from the start, trying his best to make him feel at home.

Christmas eve and the house started to take on a warm feeling with the waft of mince pies and other savoury odours that reminded one that Christmas was nigh.

"Well young Kenneth," remarked Mr. Wilson looking over his paper as they sat near the blazing log fire in the drawing room.

"It will soon be time for Santa Claus to pay you a visit. I wonder what he will bring you eh?"

Ken smiled slightly and shrugged his shoulders.

"You do believe in Santa, do you?"

"I er, I don't know sir," Ken replied quietly.

His answer made Mister Wilson put down his paper and look at Ken with some astonishment.

"Surely son, Santa must have visited you at home in Christmases past and brought you toys, chocolates and other nice things?" queried the surprised Mister Wilson.

"No sir," said Ken.

''Did you not find some thing, er... or anything different on Christmas morning?'' asked Mr. Wilson.

''Oh that sir, yes there was always a stocking, me mam's stocking hanging on the line over the fire.''

''And what may I ask, did you find in the stocking, which I presume Santa had left you?''

''There were an orange an apple, some different nuts and sometimes a block of chocolate or a selection box between us.'' Replied Ken smiling as he remembered.

''And toys?'' Mr. Wilson asked eagerly for Ken to answer in the affirmative.

''Santa did not forget to leave you some toys, surely not?''

Ken shook his head. *''I dunna think 'e ever come ter our 'ouse, cos ah Bob, 'e 's me brother, towd me, me mam put those things in 'er owd stockings.''*

A pitiful look came over Mr. Wilson's countenance, and for several moments did not speak only stared with some disbelief at the boy sitting in front of him.

''Did you ever see Santa?''

''Yes, ah saw 'im last year when 'e came ter McIlroys up 'Anley,'' replied Ken.

''And did you not speak to him and leave him a letter to tell him what toys you would like?''

A look of sorrow appeared on Ken's face.

''Ah did ner know that yer 'ad ter give 'im a letter, an' any road, me mam said 'er could ner spare a tanner fer me ter go to 'im.''

''Oh I see,'' said Mr. Wilson,

''It was sixpence to go into his grotto, was it not?''

''Yes sir, d'yer think that's wey we did'ner get any toys?''

''Perhaps, perhaps,'' beamed Mr. Wilson.

''But never you mind young Kenneth, Santa will be coming this year, I can assure you.''

''But 'ow can 'e sir? You said that yer 'ave ter send a letter, an' I anner sent one, ah did'ner know did ah?'' asked the bemused Ken.

''Ah, but you have lad,'' said Mr. Wilson, his eyes gleaming with pleasure.

''I have sent one on your behalf. What do you say to that?''

Ken looked at his benevolent host and smiled shyly. *''Thank you sir,''* he said.

''Now Kenneth, off to bed with you. We don't want to keep him waiting do we.''

It took some time for young Ken to fall asleep, he was excited for what the morrow may have in store for him. He was aroused from his sleep sometime later, and he could have sworn that he felt a weight on his legs, and in the moon light that lit the room, he saw a figure dressed in red, walking quietly across the room. This was a new experience for him, that at first made him afraid of this hooded figure, and he pulled the bed clothes over his head, then a feeling of exhilaration, that it could be no other but Santa Claus. He lay like this for some time hardly daring to breathe, then fell asleep.

He awoke next morning, Christmas day, and it was daylight. The first thing he saw was the large parcel on his legs and at the bottom of the bed a pillow, bulbous, and misshapen. Wild eyed with excitement, he jumped out of bed and carefully took the coloured wrapping paper off the parcel to reveal a box containing the largest train set he had ever seen. Hardly able to contain his joy and excitement he then examined the pillow case. This too was full of all types of toys and games. Then stepping backwards the expression on his face changed and he started to cry.

''What ever is the matter Kenneth?'' asked Mr. Wilson, who, with his wife had now entered the room.

''Why are you crying?''

Young Ken ran towards them and embraced Mrs. Wilson.

''Now, now lad, don't cry, you should be happy.''

Kenneth lifted his tearful face and looked at her.

''I, I am, I am,'' he sobbed. *''I was thinking of me sister's an' brother, an' me mam an' dad. They, they wunner 'ave owt, will thee, an' ah've 'ad o'these. It inna fair!''*

The Wilsons looked at each other and smiled. Mr. Wilson bent on one knee and pulled young Ken to him.

''What would you say if I told you that all your family are coming here to spend Christmas with us?''

''Ow, 'Ow con thee?'' he asked, his eyes opening wide and looking into the kind face of Mr. Wilson.

''Remember when I sent your letter to Santa?'' he said smiling. Ken nodded, sniffed and wiped the tears from his eyes with the back of his hand. *''Well, I also sent a letter to your parents inviting them here for Christmas, and guess what?''* Ken shook his head and started to smile.

''They have accepted and, this very morning, I have sent a car to fetch them. What do you say to that?''

Kenneth put his arms around Mr. Wilson.

''Thank you sir, an' you Missus Wilson, you're the mostest kindest people in th' world.''

''Happy Christmas son,'' said Mr. Wilson.

''A merry Christmas Kenneth'' added Mrs. Wilson.

Chapter 3
THE ONE POUND NOTE.

It was a few days before Christmas in the year 1927 A.D. Sammy Pepper was a big lad about twelve years of age. His companion, Jacky was six years old. Sammy had made arrangements with Jacky's mother to take him to the 'Penny Rush' the cinema on Saturday afternoon.

The cinema was a disused chapel situated in Cobridge, halfway between Burslem and Hanley. Just past the Granville railway crossing which fed Hanley Deep Pit with railway waggons, Jacky paused and pointed to the pavement.

"*Eh Sammy luk a pind note!*"

Sammy turned and looked at his charge and then at the pavement. A look of amazement appeared on his countenance, and in a flash pushed the lad away, grabbed the pound note and stuffed it in his pocket.

"*That's marn ah saw it fost,*" shouted Jacky.

"*It inna tharn na young un, it's marn, and ah'm keepin' it.*"

"*It's marn ah tell thee, give it us 'ere.*" With this Jacky lunged forward to beat the bigger lad on the chest with his fists.
Sammy brushed him away impatiently.

"*Ah tell thee it's marn, and if thee dustna shut up ah'll give thee a thick ear. Na, at comin' ter th' pictures or wot?*"

Jacky was by this time near to tears. He realised that Sammy was bigger and older than he, and that he would never retrieve his prize by force or any other means of persuasion.

"*Ah'll tel ah youth, ah Gud, eh'll get it off thee an gi' thee a good 'idin'.*"

"*Oh ah, 'im and oose army?*" "*At comin'ter the picture or wot?*"

"*No ah anna comin' wi' they. Theyt a thief they at. They cost goo thee sel'. Ah'm gooin' back wom an' tell ah youth!*"

The tears welled in his eyes and he started to sob.

"Goo on yer little mard arse, goo tell yo're youth eh dunna fraighten mey," Sammy shouted pushing the lad away.
Jacky stumbled and fell. He got to his feet, and clenching his fist yelled at the top of his voice at the retreating figure of Sammy, who was by this time making his way up Waterloo road to the cinema.

"They weet till ah Gudder gets thee wen thee comes wom!"

Jacky returned home with tears running down his cheeks sobbing quietly.

"Wot ever is the matter lad? Ah thote yer were gooin' ter the pictures wi' Sammy Pepper?" his mother demanded.

"Ah were," sobbed Jacky. *"Weers ah Gud?"*

"Wey, that Sammy anna 'it thee 'as 'e?"

Jacky shook his head in reply.

"Well wot cryin' fer? Someits 'appened."

"Eh's gone and pinched me one pind note eh 'as."

"Wot pind note?" she asked, her eyes widening with expectancy now that money was mentioned.

"The pind note that are funt on th' bricks up Waterloo road." Replied Jacky.

The sobbing had now ceased and was replaced by a surly angry look.

"So weer is it na?" she asked with some impatience.
"Eh's got it, that rob dog, Sammy Pepper. Eh's a thafe eh is, an'eh wunna give it ter mey".

Jacky's bottom lip curled outwards and his chin started to quiver.

"Dunna start squawking lad. Tell us wot 'appened," she said with a tone of compassion in her voice.

Jacky on the verge of another tearful outburst, related to his mother the finding of the pound note. She listened patiently until Jacky had finished. She shook her head and uttered a loud tut tut.

"Yer dozy little devil! Wot ah yer! Yer should a picked it up straight awee, shouldn't yer eh?"

Her tone had changed again to one of anger and admonishment.

"A pind note gone. Money's 'ard enough ter come by na dees wi' ite yo yer dozy devil givin' it a wee!"

"Ah couldna 'elp it." Jacky sobbed. *"Ah'm only six an' eh's bigger than mey."*

Silence ensued for several moments except for the quiet intakes of breath as Jacky fought to control his sobbing. He was an object of pity, and his mother at last responded by taking him to her breast and consoled him.

"Shush na lad, dunna fret so. Ah'll soon sort 'im ite. When will 'e back from pictures?"

"Afe past foer," Jacky answered quietly.

At half past four, she rose and taking the boy's hand in hers, made their way to the Pepper's house across the street. She was a magnificent woman some seventeen stone with arms the envy of a body builder. Heaven help the poor mortal who incurred her wrath, especially if her children and or money was involved.

She knocked at the door which was opened by Mrs. Pepper. She was not quite of the same statue as Jacky's mother but never the less, she was sturdy and no doubt she could have held her own.

"Ah belave yo've 'ad a windfo?" Jacky's mother stated in a stern matter of fact voice.

Mrs. Pepper gave a little smile of acknowledgement showing a single tooth in the centre of an otherwise toothless mouth.

"Wot d'yer mean a windfo?" she asked quietly.

"Yo know wot ah mean. 'As that lad o' yoers come wom yet?"

"Ah." Mrs. Pepper replied. *"Wot's it got ter do wi' yo'?"*

"It's got a lot ter do wi' mey. Did yoer lad give yer th' pind note that ma lad, 'im 'ere funt?"

"Yoer lad funt?" queried Mrs. Pepper.

"Ah ma lad, 'im 'ere. Eh saw it fost an' yoer lad pushed 'im ite the wee and picked it up. The young rob dog! That's wot ahm 'ere fer, me pind note that belongs ter mey!" exclaimed Jacky's mother her voice now raised, using her right arm with fist closed in a gesticulative

"Ah belave yo've 'ad a windfo?"

manner to hammer home her demand.

"It inna yoer pind note, it's marn. Ma lad picked it up fost, so it's marn. So yer know wot yo con do, dunner yer?" shouted Mrs. Pepper and at the same time started to close the door.

Jacky's mother was to quick for her. Her strong right arm shot out and held it open.

"Gis me lad's pind note or ah'll come in and tak it!"

"It inna yoers it's marn, tak yer fat arm off me dooer."

"Ah'll give yer fat arm!" Jacky's mother screamed, her face now purple with rage.

Her black hair that usually was neatly done up in a bun, had become loose and was now hanging about her face. She looked an awesome sight, wild and frightening. She raised her left fist and shook it within inches of Mrs. Pepper's face.

"Gis ma lad's pind, or ah'll let yer 'ave this in yer gob and knock that tooth ite fer yer!"

The situation had now become serious, doors were opened in the street and an audience grew. Some even dared to stand a few feet away not wishing to miss any of the entertainment. A hush and the crowd gave way to a small man dressed in black. It was Father Murphy the Catholic priest doing his pre-Christmas rounds of his wayward flock.

"Now now ladies what's to do? All this hostility and a few days before Christmas an' all an'all," he asked in a quiet Irish brogue.

Jacky's mother half turned, her fist still clenched the other hand still holding the door. Her eyes pierced his, making him step back in fear of this demented being.

"If it's any business o' yoer's," she shouted. *"This thievin' sod 'as pinched ma lads pind note."*

She had of course recognised the priest, and not being of the same denomination was not afraid of eternal damnation. The priest, gaining confidence raised his arms.

"Ladies, ladies, please tell me calmly the reason for all this rage."

"Ah've towd yer!" exclaimed Jacky's mother. *"This thievin'*

sod 'as pinched ma lad's, pind note, wot eh funt gooin' ter th' pictures, an' 'er wunna give it us back!''

''Is this right Missus....Missus Pepper isn't it. Is this right?'' Have you taken this lady's pound?''

''She's a liar she is. Ma lad, ma Sammy funt it. So it's marn!''

''Oo ah yo' coin mey a liar?'' Ah'll put this in yer toothless gob!'' shouted Jacky's Mam, raising her fist again within an inch of Mrs. Pepper's face.

''Ladies, please let us discuss this like two God fearing Catholics, sensibly and amicably.''

Jacky's mam turned and started to wave her fist under his nose.

''Fer thar information, ah anna a Catholic, ah'm a Primitive ah am, and this thievin' sod 'as pinched ma lads pind note. Ma lad saw it fost, an' 'er lad pushed 'im ite o' th' wee an' pinched it.''

By this time the priest was sandwiched between the door and the very irate Jacky's mam, her large oversized bust almost enveloping his face. With a look of stark terror in his eyes he managed, with difficulty to cross himself and mutter an Hail Mary. At last he disengaged himself and spoke with a voice he hardly recognised.

''Ladies, ladies,'' he tried hard to clear an obstruction in his throat with a cough. *''Please!''* he pleaded, *''Cannot you compromise?''*

''Comper.. wot's it. Wots mane mon?'' Jacky's mam bellowed.

The priest looked at one and then to the other, the fear in his eyes changing and a sparkle of hope began to emerge, even a suspicion of a smile appeared on his lips.

''Compromise...By this I mean.... neither of you two good ladies can agree to the valid ownership of the one pound note....''

''Ah knows oo it belongs to, it's marn!'' interrupted Jacky's mam.

''It's marn not yoer's,'' added Mrs. Pepper.

''Please, please ladies!'' exclaimed the priest, worried now that the row would flare up again.

''What I mean is, share it between you. This I'm sure would be

the only solution... ten shillings each''.

Silence ensued for several moments, the two women dead in thought.

''Well?'' he asked. *''Well?''*

''Ah wull, if 'er wull,'' Jacky's mam replied.

The priest looked at Mrs. Pepper, willing her to answer in the affirmative.

''Ah o'raight then, if it'll stop o' this mither,'' she replied.

She half turned and shouted into the house:

''Sammy, bring us me poss off the shelf.''

A few seconds later the purse was delivered into her hands and she extracted the one pound note.

'' 'Ave yer got ten bob?'' she asked Jacky's mam.

''Ah anna got ten bob, weer d'yer think ah've got ten bob on a Saturdee naight?''

''Please allow me,'' the priest said hurriedly in case the row would start up again.

He withdrew from his inside pocket, a worn brown wallet from which he extracted two ten shilling notes. One he gave to Jacky's mam, the other to Mrs. Pepper at the same time relieving her of the pound note.

''There ladies,'' he said with a smile. *''That solved the problem did it not? A very happy Christmas to you both.''*

'' Ah still see it wer ma lad's pound note, eh funt it fost, and it shudder bin 'is.''

With this she took Jacky by the hand, crossed the street, turned and shouted:

''An' the same ter yo ah'm sure.''

Jacky awoke early on Christmas morning, excited with the expectation of Santa's visit. His mother's old lyle stocking was hanging on the line that crossed the old range. It was bulbous, misshapen, and he took it down eager to discover its contents. His mother sat at the table drinking a cup of tea.

''Eh's bin then, Santa's bin,'' she said with a twinkle in her

eyes.

Jacky quickly emptied the contents of the stocking on to the table. Two oranges, two apples, a variety of nuts, and quite a few caramels. His face lit up when his mother handed him another gift, wrapped up neatly in red coloured tissue paper. *"Goo on open it,"* she said.

He opened it carefully not wishing to damage the covering.

"Mam!" he exclaimed. *"Luk a afe pind o' fruit an' nut chocolate. Mam..int Christmas great? Int Santa good? O this."*

His eyes gleamed with joy and happiness.

"Ah," she sighed. *"If yer anna bin ser dozy a few dees agoo, wen yer funt that pind note, an' let 'im 'ave it across the wee, mebbe Santa would o' left yer a 'ole pind block instead of only afe a pind."*

Chapter 4
YANKS FOR THE MEMORY

A long time ago, some over half a century since a mighty war waged throughout Europe and most of the world. A flurry of snow descended on the blacked out streets of Hanley. A single torch light sheared through the velvety blackness like a silver sword. An irate warning from a voice reverberated through the night.

"Put that light out!"

Like magic the beam of light vanished. The torch bearer muttering incoherently groping her way through the darkness. The door opened at the Port Vale public house allowing a blur of light to be cast upon the pavement, and shadowy figures in strange uniforms emerged laughing and shouting. Six or more American soldiers now in high spirits, their cigarettes and cigars glowing in their hands and lips like fire flies. The door to the hostelry opened wider still emitting more light on the scene allowing three drunken revellers to pass through.

"Put that light out! Shut that door!" the loud angry voice of the unseen sentinel demanded.

"Up yours Mac!" replied one of the Yanks.

They lounged by the pub windows laughing and trying to attract the young ladies passing by with wolf whistles and offers of candies, cigarettes and nylons. One of them started to sing. He had a fair voice though slurred somewhat by the alcohol he had imbibed earlier.

"Silent Night, Holy Night."

After the first verse the others joined in unison, in protest perhaps to the A.R.P warden's request or the fact that Christmas day would be with them in just two days time.

Ada was a buxom lass of nineteen. She was returning home after working on the afternoon shift at Shelton Bar. Her job was hard having replaced a man who had been called up for the army. In normal times she would not have been considered for this work, for it was heavy,

Stafford Street, Hanley

hard and dirty.

She put the torch in her pocket and she walked slowly passed the Port Vale pub and the crowd of the singing G.I's. One by one they accosted her offering her bribes and sweet talk. She was weary and eager to get home, trying her utmost to ignore them. She thought she had succeeded, and by the time she had reached Brown's the butchers she had dismissed all of them with the exception of one who was more persistent. He was tall and quite heavily built, and he took hold of Ada's arm and put it in his.

''Please,'' she implored. *''Let go my arm.''*

''But baby I wanna take you home,'' he slobbered.

''Now look Yank, if yer dunner let goo of me arm, they't bey carried wom on a stretcher!'' retorted Ada.

Whether he did not comprehend the colloquial dialect we shall never know, but he started to laugh and hold her tighter. By this time they had reached the little entry between Dolcis shoe shop and Joan's Gowns shop. This had been made into a temporary air raid shelter with sandbags.

''Come on baby be nice to Hank,'' with this he tried to pull Ada into the shelter.

''Raight Yank, they'st asked fer it!''

She twisted him around with the arm he was holding until he was facing her. There appeared on his countenance a very surprised look. Never before in all his amorous advances to the opposite sex, had he been subjected thus. Then Ada delivered the 'coup de gras', a right cross which landed on his jaw. The Yank's eyes glazed over and he fell backwards onto the sandbags and slithered to the ground as though he had been pole-axed. Ada, hands on hips, stood over him triumphantly.

''Well Yank ah did warn yer!'' she exclaimed, turned on her heels and walked away.

The next day, Christmas Eve, Ada sat in the rolling mill with her workmate Hilda eating their snap contemplating the two days holiday, and discussing what they were going to do over Christmas.

''Yo' goo past the Port Vale pub on yer wee wom, dunner yer Ada?'' asked Hilda stuffing the remains of a Spam sandwich into her mouth.

''Ah. Wey?'' queried Ada.

''Thee were a spot o' bother theer last naight at closin' tarme, so ah wer towd. Ah thote yo' wudder sayne it.''

Ada shook her head and filled the enamel mug with tea from her Billy Can.

''Wey wot 'appened?''

''Well, wot 'Arry 'Ancock. Yer know 'Arry dunner yer? Works on the blast furnace, a mate of your Jack's afer 'e joined up.''

''Ah, I know 'im,'' answered Ada. *'' 'Im that married Elsie wot's 'er name from up Paddocks Strate.''*

"Ah that's 'im," affirmed Hilda taking another sandwich from her tin snapping box. *"Well eh said, 'Arry said thee were a raight ter do. Wi' yankee bobbies wi' wate 'elmets an'sticks an'guns. Ah bobbies as well, then a ambulance come. Thee were Yanks all o'er th' place. 'Arry said the perlice 'ad towd 'im that a Yank 'ad bin beaten up an' were unconscious wi' blood all o'er th' place. Thee put Yank on a stretcher an' put 'im in th' ambulance still ite cowd. 'Arry said 'eh'd bin set upon by....Guess oo?"*

Ada, the mug of tea raised to her lips, a ghost of a smile on her face. *"No. Oo?"* she asked.

"A woman!" Hilda exclaimed with excitement and amazement. *"Ah it's raight. A Woman! 'Arry 'eard 'em see that they were after a big woman abite seventain stoon. 'Arry said th' perlice cowd 'er 'The Lady wi' th' Limp an' a warrant 'ad bin put ite fer 'er arrest fer grevious bodily 'arm. An' ter mak things woss, 'er'd bin sayne by witnesses. Yanks oo wer standin' theer by th'pub, saw 'er wen th' dooer opened."*

Ada had started to swallow the tea, but hearing that she was a wanted woman, the mechanism in her throat went haywire, and her unfortunate mate, being in direct line was showered by hot sweet tea.

"Ada! Yer dirty devil yo'!" exclaimed Hilda wiping herself on a piece of rag that was on a bench nearby. Then a look of enlightenment and a big smile came over her face.

"It wer yo. Wanna it? Eh wanna it?"

Ada now composed herself. Nodded and started to laugh. *"Serve the bugger raight. That'll teach 'im not ter molest married women in future."*

"If ah were yo'," remarked Hilda, now doubled up with laughter. "If *ah were yo.... ah'd try not ter limp wi' that leg... that yer 'urt t'other dee."*

Ada did try not to walk with a limp that night on her way home, and took a different route so as to miss the Port Vale pub and the G.I's.

The incident faded from her mind for, on reaching home, there was her Jack, her husband on a seven day furlough.

"Merry Christmas me bonny lass." Taking her in his arms and kissing her.

"Well Yank ah did warn yer!"

"Merry Christmas ter yo Jack," she replied.

"When d'yer goo back?"

"Owd on, giz me tarme ter get me feet under th' table, ah've only just got 'ere. Dun yer want ter get rid of me. Yo anna got one o' those Yanks in tow 'ave yer?" Jack said smiling.

Ada blushed, if only he knew she thought. *"Ah resent that Jack. yer've no right ter say that!"*

"Ah wer only joking duck, ah know yo better than that ah know yer wudner get mixed up wi' them. Yer know wot thee say abite em dunner yer?"

"No wot?" she asked.

"Over sexed an' over 'ere, any road ah've got seven dees leave.

So termorrer naight get thee glad rags on.''

''Oh ah, wey?''

''Some of me mates an' the waives wi us ah 'avin a naight ite on th' town''

''That'll be nice Jack, weer we gooin'?''

''Port Vale pub up 'Anley,'' replied Jack.

''Pport Vale?'' Ada stammered.

''Ah,'' replied Jack looking at her with suspicion. *''Wey wot's up wi' Port Vale?''*

Ada was now in a bit of a dilemma. What could she do? What could she say. To tell him what happened would really upset the apple cart and spoil his few days at home. There was also the warrant out for her arrest. She would surely be recognised.

''I anna gooin' in theer,'' she said at last. *''Thee'll be nowt but trouble.''*

''Wey will they bey trouble?'' asked Jack.

''Cos'' Ada hesitated. *''Cos the place is full o' Yanks, yer know wot 'appens wen yo lot an' Yanks mix thase o' wees trouble. So if it's o' th' same ter yo' ah'm stoppin'at wom. Yo' con please yer sel!''*

Chapter 5
CHRISTMAS HOT POT

The room was cold and dark. A few embers of coal in the black range gave no comfort at all. The room was sparsely furnished; a table the top well scrubbed, a large wooden armchair, a kitchen chair and a wooden settle. A woman in her early thirties sat sobbing and a young boy no more than ten was holding her hand trying his best to console her.

"If only he'd come home," she sobbed. *"He must have finished work hours ago. Christmas eve and ah've nothing in the house. Nothing at all!"*

"Ah bet 'e'll be in the pub swillin' beer down 'im. 'E couldna' care less about us," the boy said.

There was hatred in his voice there was also fear.

"Ah'll go and see if ah con find 'im mam."

He was clad in an old shirt that had been patched so many times that no vestige of the original remained. The trousers reaching to his knees were also patched. He wore no stockings on his legs and on his feet a pair of old worn clogs.

"All right son, but put your jacket on, it's bitterly cold outside."

The jacket was no better than the rest of his apparel, worn and threadbare. He lifted the latch to the door, and made his way along Bryan Street. The wind was keen and a few flakes of snow showed white against the gas lamps now being lit by the lamplighter who flitted like a moth from one lamp to another. The boy turned up the collar of his jacket and then dug his hands deep into the pockets. His first call was the Crown and Anchor at the corner of New Hall Street and Foundry Street. He had a good idea where his father's watering places were. The warmth and the smell of tobacco smoke and beer made him feel giddy as he looked around the room for his errant parent. Dozens of bleary eyes met his.

A loud rasping voice:-" *Close that blasted door,* " made him jump and he departed quickly leaving the door to close slowly on its own. He quickly walked along Stafford street and entered the Port Vale. The same scene again but still no parent. He walked up Lamb street to the market square which was alive with activity. Bands, buskers', a man singing and salesmen all competing with each other. The 'Hot Potato' man was doing a roaring trade, and he envied his customers' and yearned to hold and taste the hot roasted delicacy. He shivered with the cold and the snow flakes flurried about him. Sinking his head further into his jacket collar and burying his hands deeper into his pockets, he heard the rumble of his stomach and felt its emptiness reminding him that the only meal he had eaten that day, was a small basin of porridge, and a piece of bread and dripping.

He walked quickly across the street to avoid the tram that noisily approached him. He stood momentarily at the large door of the Angel Hotel daring himself to enter its portals. He had heard his father say, in one of his rare sober moments, that it was the largest bar in the city.

He opened the door slowly and the cacophony of sound overwhelmed him. There was singing and shouting, glasses clattered on the marble top of the bar, the till bell rung merrily bringing happiness to the proprietor's ear. A shrill burst of ladies laughter, a hearty roar of laughter from some toper in the far corner, raised voices of argument from one of the booths, and above the heads a pall of blue smoke and the aroma of cheap cigars. The whole scene frightened him and he was about to leave when he saw a man that he recognised, a neighbour. He pulled at the man's sleeve to gain his attention.

''Excuse me Mister Davies, ccould yyer?'' he asked nervously.

The man looked down at the boy.

''Yes lad? Oh it's young Jackie, Sam Jackson's lad. Wot are yer doin' in 'ere son?''

He smiled and put his hand on the boy's shoulder.

''C'mon lad dunna be fraightened, wot's want?''

Jackie felt better now encouraged by the man's warmth.

''Could yer please tell me if me faither's in 'ere?''

Bill Davies looked down the room.

''Ah 'e is lad, ah saw 'im just a few minutes agoo. Dust want me get 'im fer thee?''

Jackie nodded.

''Stay thee 'ere lad an' ah'll go and see if ah con find 'im.''

Bill disappeared amongst the crowd reappearing a few moments with Jackie's father following behind him. Jackie could see that his father was the worse for wear, his unshaven face was flushed and he walked with a reeling motion. He was large and muscular, no doubt due to his work as a navvy. He was still dressed in his working clothes, and the smell of earth, beer, sweat and tobacco pervaded from his person.

He stopped and looked down at the boy swaying as he spoke:

''Wot's they want in 'ere?''

Young Jackie looked up at him with fear in his eyes.

''Ah said, wot's want?''

''Mmme mmam,'' he stuttered his lower lip starting to tremble.

''Mme mmam wants ter know wen are yer ccomin' 'ome?''

Sam Jackson's face took on another darker hue and snarled through his tobacco stained teeth: *"Oh she does, does she! Ah'll teach yer ter come maitherin' mey!"*

With this he struck the lad across the head which floored him, then he bent down and lifted him up to the level of his face.

"Tell thee mother that ah'll bay comin' wom wen it suits may."

He dropped the boy on to the floor who landed on one knee and with one hand over his head to protect himself from any further blows.

He whimpered pitifully.

"Na sod off an' dunna bother may agen!"

He was about to strike the boy again when Bill intervened.

"There's no need fer that Sam!"

The bully shook himself free from Bill's grip.

"Oh ah!" he snarled. *"An' wot the 'ell as it got ter do wi' yo'?"*

"Ah dunna lark ter see a young lad knocked abite fer nowt," Bill Davies answered.

He was calm but his eyes steeled and his face paled.

"They dustna dust?" Jackson put his face close to Bill's and started to prod him in the chest with his finger.

"Way want none o' that in 'ere. Pack it in or ite yer goo!" An' get that lad ite o' 'ere befer ah 'ave the perlice on me back," shouted the loud menacing voice from the proprietor from the other side of the bar.

One of Sam Jackson's drinking cronies led him away before an affray started for he was in an ugly mood and was ready to take on all the men in the bar for it was well known that in the past, it had taken quite a few of the Hanley constabulary to quell his savagery, and put him in cells for the night. Jackson had received a good payout that day and it was Christmas, and his cronies wanted their share to spend in ale and not for their benefactor to languish in the towns lock-up during the festive season.

Bill Davies finished drinking his beer and walked out. Young Jackie was just outside crying.

He took his hand. *"Come on son let me take you 'ome,"* he said quietly and with compassion.

Jackie lay awake most of the night awaiting for his father's homecoming, for he was afraid what he might do to his mother in his drunken rage. It wouldn't be the first time he had kept awake and trembled with fear and anger by the drunkard's brutal assaults on his poor mother. Oh how he wished and prayed that he was strong enough to protect her. One day he vowed that he would be.

He heard his mother sobbing and he pressed his hands to his ears to try and obliterate the heart rending sound. Dawn was breaking and the room took on a greyness, and he was able to perceive his little sister who shared the same bed with him. Jackie at the top and his sister Alice, at the bottom. The only covering was a grey blanket and an old army great coat. It was Christmas Day, but there would be no visit from Santa Claus or stockings full of toys for these two. They would be indeed lucky if they received anything to eat.

His father had not come home, and he felt easier now, and relaxed, and in a few moments he was fast asleep. He was awakened by his mother gently shaking him, and startled, he jumped up.

"*It's all right son it's only me,*" she said.

Jackie reassured, nodded and rubbed his eyes with his fists.

"*Did me dad come 'ome mam?*" he asked.

"*No*" she answered. "*I don't know what's happened to him. Still it's not the first time and I don't think it will be the last. Come lad have your breakfast, for what it is.*"

The breakfast was as usual a small bowl of porridge and a piece of bread and dripping. The room was cold because there was no fire burning in the grate.

"*'Ow did yer manage ter make the oats mam?*" Jackie asked.

"*I'd a penny left so I put in the gas.*"

"*When ah've finished this I'll go on the shard ruck and pick some cinders.*"

She nodded and picked up the little girl to give her some warmth from her body. A tear slowly fell from her eye and her lower lip trembled.

"*What ever is going to become of us,*" she thought trying hard to keep her distress from the children.

A knock on the door. Jackie had finished his meagre meal and went to see who it was. Bill Davies stood there smiling.

"Is yer dad in son"? he asked.

"No Mister Davies."

"Who is it Jackie?" his mother asked from the living room.

"It's me Missus, Bill Davies from along the street, ah wanted a word with your Sam like."

"I'm sorry he's not in."

"Come in fer a minute Mister Davies," invited Jackie.

"Ah 'o'raight son, just fer a minute."

Bill Davies was appalled how poverty stricken the place was, how cold. Mrs. Jackson was clearly embarrassed at their predicament.

"You 'eard from young Jackie ah suppose that me and Sam 'ad a few words last naight?"

"Yes," she answered quietly. *"I feel so ashamed."*

She took an handkerchief out of her apron pocket and held it to her mouth. Bill started to fidget passing his cap from one hand to the other.

"Yer see ah wanted ter 'ave a word with 'im this mornin' while 'e were sober like. Ah like things straight yer know, cards on table like."

"I'm sorry, I would like to thank you for looking after young Jackie"

"Dunna mention it missus, ah couldna' stand by an' see the lad knocked abite fer nowt."

The cold was getting to him and he pointed at the empty grate.

"Yer'll excuse me missus, but 'ave yer no coal"?

She did not answer but shook her head.

"Ah shanna bay a minute." Bill turned and was gone.

Mrs. Jackson started to cry.

"Dunna cry mam."

Young Jackie walked over to her and put his arm around her. Another knock on the door and it opened and Bill Davies walked in carrying a large bucket of coal, some paper and sticks.

"Yer'll excuse me lettin me sel' in."

He put the coal, sticks and paper on the hearth. Taking up the poker cleaned out the few ashes in the grate, set the fire and lit it. In a few moments he had the fire blazing.

"That's better eh? Come on Missus bring the young lass and yo Jackie get nearer the fire and get yersel's warm. It's Christmas Dee!"

He smiled and the room took on a warm glow.

"Fer ah ferget," he took from his pocket two blocks of chocolate and gave one to the girl and one to the boy. They were not used to receiving presents and were slow to accept them.

"Goo on, tak' em," Bill said.

The two children smiled and looked at their mother as though asking her permission. She nodded and smiled.

"Now Missus wot about yer dinner"?

The smile disappeared and she shrugged her shoulders.

"Yer know missus, ah lost ma good lady nearly two year agoo and ahm on me own, there wouldna be nowt nicer than yo' an' the two children ter come an' spend Christmas wi' mey. But it wouldna be raight some 'ow, so ah anna gooin ter ask yer. But ah would like ter know, 'ave yer no dinner?"

"No," she answered softly.

"Wot about yer 'ot pot?" he asked.

"Hot pot. What Hot pot?"

"Did yer not read abite it in th'Sentinel?"

"No we can't afford a paper."

"Well the business people, trader's and better off, are givin' away ter needy folk lark yersel' free 'ot pots."

"But I don't like," she said softly then straightening her back in a defiant gesture, *"I wont accept charity!"*

"Dunna bay silly. It inna charity, it's a free gift from the better off, their wee o' sayin' Merry Christmas ter the poor and needy. So put on yer 'at and coot and let's 'ave yer up the market. Yer wont be the only one, ther'll be lots o' folk fetchin' the 'ot pot this mornin'."

She rose slowly and went behind the parlour door where she kept her clothes. She did not possess a hat and coat only an old shawl which she put over her shoulders.

''Are you sure they are free?'' she asked with a shyness in her voice.

''Course ah'm sure,'' Bill said with a smile.

''Now bey off wi' yer and ah'll stop wi' the kids till yer come back. And, if that 'usband o' yours comes in we con 'ave words private like. Dunna ferget yer basins, yer'll want thray good sized ones. 'ave yer got some?''

With the three basins she left, feeling happier now, knowing the children would be able to eat, and another feeling that she just could not comprehend. Her thoughts were of this knight in shining armour, his kindness and understanding.

She was soon at the Market hall and there were hundreds of women all bent on the same errand forming a queue. The ladies behind the trestles smiling benevolently, filling the proffered basins from the large stainless steel containers. An aroma of well cooked, well flavoured food filled the hall. Mrs. Jackson carefully balanced the well filled basins against her body.

''Can you manage love?'' asked one of the helpers. She nodded and with a thank you hurried home.

Bill Davies was still there reading a story from an old book. Young Alice was sitting on his knee and Jackie was sitting at his feet in front of the blazing fire eating the chocolate and listening intently to every word. She entered the room and placed the three basins on the table.

''Yer've got 'em then. No trouble?'' Bill got up from the chair and gently sat Alice in the chair.

''Yes,'' she answered. *''Thank you very much Mister Davies. I had no trouble at all, the ladies were very nice''*

''Well I'll be going now, but I'll be along later to see if you're alright''

He turned to go. And just before he went through the door he

"Can you manage love?"

said: *"Merry Christmas."*

He smiled and was gone.

The Hot Pots were delicious and were thoroughly enjoyed by the family.

"Mam," said Jackie smiling. *"That were lovely, ah'm full."*

"Yes it was son, very nice."

Little Alice smiled broadly and murmured, *"Mmm."*

"Thanks to kind mister Davies and all the people, all those

good people who gave them and there time. God Bless them.''

''Isn't mister Davies a nice man mam? Ah wish 'e were me dad.''

True to his word, Bill returned at tea time with another bucket of coal, a large tin of pineapple chunks, a tin of cream, a cake, a loaf of bread, a packet of butter and a ham. He placed the fare on the table.

''Ah've brote a few things for your tea,'' he said.

''Oh mister Davies you shouldn't. You've been too good already,'' she replied, her eyes lighting up.

She seemed very happy and he too was pleased to see her like this.

''Missus, I'm only too pleased to be doing this, it gives me great pleasure to be sharing it with yer. Ah've no one ter share it with. Ah only wish it were in different circumstances,'' he paused then with concern in his voice: *'''E's still not come 'ome yet?''*

She shook her head and bit her bottom lip.

''Well never mind,'' he said with a smile, *''Let's be 'avin this tea and, if yer dunna mind ah'll be joinin' yer.''*

The next morning, Boxing day, there was a knock on the door. Jackie opened it and two large men were standing there. One a police constable, and another in plain clothes.

''Is yer mam in son?''

Jackie stepped back, a feeling of foreboding came over him. He nodded and answered *''Yes.''*

''Well goo and tell 'er we want ter see 'er, that's a good lad,'' the one in the plain clothes said.

''Mam!'' Jackie shouted. *''There's somebody wants ter see yer.''*

She came immediately her mouth wide and a look of apprehension on her face.

''Yes?'' She asked softly.

The man in the plain clothes, touched his bowler hat.

''Are you missus Jackson?'' he asked.

''I am.''

She put her arm around Jackies shoulder hoping he would be able to support her when they informed her of the bad news she guessed they bore.

"Can we come in?" he asked.

"Yes, yer can", she turned still holding on to her son and made her way to the living room, and sat down on a chair.

The two men followed her. The constable took a note book from his tunic pocket.

"I'm Detective sergeant Buller and this is police constable Walker," the man in the plain clothes said.

"I'm sorry ter 'ave ter inform yer, but ah've got some bad news."

"It's my husband, Sam, isn't it"?

She took up little Alice who had been sitting on the floor and held her on her knee then drew Jackie to her as though to protect them from some unseen danger.

"I'm afraid so," answered the detective. He coughed and straightened his shoulders to prepare him self to deliver the grave news. *"We 'ave this mornin' taken a mans body from the canal in Etruria. We've reason ter believe it was your 'usband."*

"But how do you know it's Sam?" she asked.

"We found on 'is person a wage packet with 'is name on it. It was empty I'm afraid, and we've reason ter believe there was foul play involved and 'e 'ad bin robbed."

She lowered her head and started to cry. No one spoke for several moments, then Jackie put his arm around her shoulders.

"When, when did yer see yer 'usband last missus Jackson?"

She took an handkerchief from her pocket wiped the tears from her eyes and quietly blew her nose.

"Christmas Eve morning when he went to work," she replied.

"And yer've not seen 'im since?"

She shook her head. *"No but young Jackie here saw him that night."*

"Oh did yer lad. And weer was that?"

''*The Angel public 'ouse up 'anley*'', Jackie answered with some trepidation.

''*And wot were yer doin' in there me lad*''? asked the detective.

''*I sent him to find his dad, because I wanted some money to buy food,*'' she said and she started to sob again.

''*Oh, and did 'e, yer 'usband, do this often?*''

''*What?*'' She asked.

''Goo drinkin' and leave yer 'wi' ite any money?''

She nodded and lowered her head on her breast as if in shame.

''*And Jackie, wot did yer dad say wen yer found 'im eh.*''?

He looked at his mother and she gave her permission with a nod.

'' *'E were drunk and 'e 'it me and said ter tell me mam 'e'd come wom when it suited 'im.*''

''*An' wot appened next?*'' asked the detective.

'' *'E were gooin' ter 'it me agen, but mister Davies stopped 'im.*''

''*Oh, an' oose mister Davies?*''

Jackie again looked at his mother for support.

''*Mister Davies is a neighbour, lives just along the street. He's a very kind gentleman. If it had not been for him I don't know what we would have done this Christmas.*''

Detective Buller laid his hand on Jackie's shoulder. A half smile on his face.

''*Did this nice mister Davies and yer dad come ter blows lad?*''

Jackie shrugged the mans hand off his shoulder in defiance.

''*No! 'E just stopped me faither 'ittin' me agen, and this other man come and took me faither awee!*''

''*Did yer know this other man lad?*''

''*No.*''

''*Will yer tell the constable wot number mister Davies lives at Jackie?*''

Detective Buller turned to the constable.

''*Wen the lad's towd thee the number goo and see 'im and ask 'im ter accompany you ter the station. Yer con tell 'im wot it's abite and we would like 'im ter 'elp us with ah inquiries and ah'll see yer later at the station.''*

The constable took the number off Jackie then left.

''Ah'm sorry Missus but ah must ask yer come wi' me.''

''Wot for?'' she asked apprehensively.

The detective held up his hand in an effort to calm her.

''Na Missus dunna upset yer sel'. It's just a matter of identification, not a nice job ah know, but it's got ter be done. 'Ave yer got a neighbour ter look after the children?''

''I will have no neighbours in my house. My lad will look after the young one.''

She looked at Jackie. *''Will you be alright son?''*

He took her hand in his and nodded.

''Course we will mam. Dunna worry.''

She got to her feet and put her shawl around her shoulders.

''Anna yer got a coot? It's cowd ite side,'' the detective asked.

She shook her head and they left. An hour later, after the harrowing ordeal of identifying the body of her husband and more questions by the police, she returned home. Neighbours stopped her in the street and offered their condolences, some hoping to get the news first hand instead of reading about it in the Sentinel. After all it was their tragedy too. It wasn't every day they found a body in the canal who had died in mysterious circumstances, somebody they knew any way. Bill Davies was not so fortunate and was treated as the number one suspect, due to his involvement with the family and from the outset, detective Buller suspected that this was a 'crime passionnel', and poor Bill, his reward for all his good intentions, was interrogated for several hours then remanded in custody.

Later, the same night, the police were informed by the proprietor of the Angel Hotel, that two men who had been drinking with Sam Jackson on Christmas Eve, were now in the bar and had been drinking heavily. Detective Sergeant Buller and three constables were at once despatched to the hotel, and ordered the two men to go with them to Hanley police station to assist them with their inquiries. They became argumentative then violent, and after a fierce struggle were overcome by the police. They were questioned all night and in the early hours of the next day, they finally broke down and in their drunken stupor tried blaming each other. They confessed to assaulting and robbing Sam Jackson on the towpath near to the Etruria Inn, in which public house they finished their drunken orgy after leaving the Angel Hotel. The two miscreants, by name, Riley and Hogan, were adamant that Jackson was alive though unconscious when they left him by the canal. It was later confirmed by the Pathologist, that death was due to drowning but severe bruising to the face and body showed that he had been severely assaulted before his death.

The two itinerant navvies were remanded in custody to await trial. Bill Davies was released, and his first call he made was to see his adopted family. They all welcomed him and, time being a great healer, their love and affection for each other grew. Six months after the tragedy, Bill asked Mrs. Jackson if she would become his wife. She of course consented, and young Jackie, his wish now fulfilled, was happy to call him 'Dad'.

Chapter 6
SPIRITS OF RETRIBUTION.

Never before had this sense of foreboding been so strong in all his working years as a collier. It seemed to envelope his very soul. He embraced his wife passionately not wanting to let go.

"You'll be late Jack," she whispered.

"Aye", he said sadly.

He turned and took in his arms his two small children and kissed them gently.

"Bye", he said and carefully placed them on the wooden settle.

With one last look at his family he opened the door and made his way to the pit.

Jack, stripped to the waist was hewing coal. The dim light of his lamp hanging on a roof support reflected the perspiration on his body. His loader, a youth of eighteen was busy loading the hewed coal into a tub. The usual sound of pick and shovel against coal was interrupted when a lad of fourteen came running panic stricken into the stall.

"Quick, let's get out, water's broken in!"

Jack paused in his task and looked askance at the lad, and even in the dim light could see the terror in his eyes. He realised at once that this was no practical joke that lads of this age are prone to do, and also this feeling of foreboding that was still within him. Taking his lamp he told the two to follow him.

"Let's make it to the pit bottom as quick as we can!"

Reaching the main dip, he was astonished by the scene. The water was like a swollen river as from a breached dam, pouring with intense fury tearing and bringing everything in its path, tubs, timber, even the rails off the roads. In the light of their lamps they could see that only a few yards down the dip the water was now as high as the roof.

"Is there no other way out Jack?" asked Harry the loader.

"Are we going to die?" asked Billy, who at that moment started

sob.

Jack put his hand on his shoulder. *"Not if I can help it lad, let's make it to Bourne's crut and down the air road to the upcast shaft".*

They moved quickly and within a few minutes reached the heavy doors to the return air road and opened them. Their hopes were dashed for the scene was the same as the main dip. They were cut off. A new danger then at that moment presented itself, the oil lamps began to flicker.

"Gas!" Jack exclaimed. *"Close the doors quick!"*

A feeling of despondency overcame him, for he knew that if the water did not reach them in time the gas would. Immediately he realised that he must be brave for the sake of the younger ones in his care.

"We'll make for the highest place and wait for the water to stop and go down. Don't worry lads we'll soon be out of here. I bet they've got the pumps goin' like the Billy-oh," Jack assured them with a smile.

They huddled together, waiting. It took about an hour for the water to reach them. Young Billy started to cry and Jack put his arm around him and this calmed him.

"Jack, what's caused all this water to come?"

"Greed lad, the owner of the pit's greed", replied Jack.

"What do you mean"?

"There's an old pit that flooded years ago called the Heaton. 57 men perished. I were a lad at the time and my Dad was in it and still is they never got 'em out. The owner of this pit was warned that he must keep a barrier of coal between this pit and that to act as a sort of a dam. I saw him and the manager arguing about the boundary a few weeks ago. I heard the owner Quigley, tell him he wanted that coal and that he would have it despite the consequences. He did and you know the result lad. I only hope he lives with this on his conscience till the day he dies. Curse him! And let him rot in Hell!"

The water by this time had reached their knees and was rising slowly.

"I think lads it's time we said a prayer," said Jack.

Young Billy started to sob again and lifted his tear stained face. *"I, I don't want to die Jack, not like this"*

"No lad. A prayer will help."

"Jack, I'm frightened," Harry murmured. *"Will... Will it take long?"*

"No Harry. Take hold of my hand... O Lord we beseech thee in this our hour of need. To give us courage and deliver us from this watery tomb. If thy will be done, keep our families in thy loving care. Sustain them O Lord in their hours of grief....."

"I, I don't want to die Jack, not like this"

Before he could continue the icy cold black water had reached their waists, the lamps flared and went out. The gas had been forced up to them.

"Mother! Mother!" Billy screamed and clung to Jack.

There was light all around that was ethereal, a feeling of peace and tranquillity. A man appeared before them dressed in a white robe.

"Jack," whispered young Billy.

"Yes Lad?" answered Jack.

"Where are we? Have we been saved? Whose the man in white?"

"I er... don't know lad," replied Jack in a subdued voice.

At last the man in white spoke:

"Do not be afraid. I have been sent to look after you."

"Bbut," stuttered Harry, *"Where are we, have we been rescued, or are we d..... Dead?"*

"We prefer to say passed over," the man in white replied smiling.

"Passed over?" asked Harry. *"What do you mean?"*

"You were not rescued from that flooded mine. You, all of you are in a kind of limbo. You see we are not ready for you yet, there were so many of you. You have been chosen the three of you for a special task."

"We still don't understand. We are either dead or alive. What do you mean we've been chosen for a special task?" Jack asked.

"I know you must be very confused. Yes you did lose your earthly lives in that terrible pit. Has I have said we prefer to say passed over. You are to return for a short period of time to right things that have befallen you and your fellow men. Your spirits will be seen and heard by one man only. You will of course visit your relatives to say good bye. This will happen two days before the eve of Christmas."

Jack found himself in familiar surroundings, his humble cottage. Mary, his wife was sitting by the table her head in her arms sobbing. By the oil lamp on the table Jack could see a piece of paper before her. He moved to her side and put his hand on her shoulder to comfort her. She did not respond to his touch and Jack was full of compassion for her.

"Oh if only she could see and hear me," he cried.

Looking down at the paper on the table he read the spidery handwriting: -

Mrs. Meeson, I hereby give you two weeks notice

to quit the cottage. Terminating January 12th 1910.
I will need this cottage for another collier and his family.
Signed.
A. Quigley. Owner.

A wave of anger overcame him, a vehement desire for revenge obsessed his very soul.

"Has the man no compassion, no conscience. How can he inflict all this anguish on his fellow man," he wailed.
The man in the white robe appeared at his side.

"Calm yourself. The time for retribution will come," he said.

In a few moments the rage abated, and he again put his hand on the shoulder of his wife.

"I know that you cannot hear me or see me my love, but I am here at your side and I will be until eternity."

He went to the bedroom to his two small children, lying together, serene, oblivious to what fate had in store for them.

"Come now, my son, let peace be with you," spoke the man in the white robe. *"We have other work to do. For you are to right the evil that has befallen you and your comrades."*

Jack was now joined by the spirits of Harry and Billy in different surroundings, a large dark cold baronial building. The home of Quigley the colliery owner. It had now started to snow and the wind howled. A dim light showed in one of the many windows on an upper floor.

"The man you are to meet is an evil greedy man, with no compassion for his fellow man, he is the owner of several collieries and his God is gold. It is your task, the reason you have been allowed to remain on this earthly plain, to make him denounce his evil ways and to right some of the sadness and despair he has caused. He and he alone will be able to see and hear you."

On saying this the man in the white robe left them.

The trio entered the room still attired in their pit clothes. Water dripped from them on the carpeted floor. Jack's anger returned on seeing the man responsible for all the suffering. His eyes glared and he started to approach the desk where the man sat engrossed in looking at some plan of underground workings. The candle on the desk flickered and he looked up in alarm at the three apparitions.

"*Who are you? What do you want? How did you get in here?*" he croaked.

Jack's anguish increased when he thought of his family and he started to wail. Quigley in alarm fell backwards off his chair and lay cringing on the floor. The colour had drained from his face and was now a deadly white. His hair in that moment had gone white.

"*We are the spirits of the men you murdered and the countless others who have suffered and died through your greed,*" Jack cried.

"*We are the spirits of retribution!*"

"*Mercy! Have mercy!*" Quigley pleaded." I *have not murdered anyone!*"

He was now on his knees his hands clasped together as though in prayer.

"*This plan,*" replied Jack pointing to the plan on the desk.

"*You were warned not to take coal from there, but through your greed you released water from the old Heaton pit and a score and more men and boys perished.*"

"*I know that now, please forgive me,*" he mumbled pathetically. "*Bbut I had to have that coal, don't you see?*" He looked at the three in turn his ashen face contorted with fear, his eyes searching desperately for a sign of pity. "*Yes, so I could find you work to feed your families, I had to take the gamble.....Have mercy..... Have pity... Please!*"

"*My wife,*" Jack was calmer now, "*my wife and children will have to spend their days in the workhouse. This boy,*" he continued pointing at young Billy, "*was the only breadwinner who cared for his father who was crippled in one of your pits. What will become of him?*"

Quigley's shoulders heaved with sobbing, "*What do you intend to do with me?*" he whimpered.

"*We intend to stay and haunt you for the rest of your miserable life....That is unless....''*

''Yes. Unless?'' Quigley pleaded. *''Anything.''*

''Tomorrow,'' Jack said, *''Is the Eve of Christmas, you will visit all the dependants of this disaster and make amends for all the misery you have caused them. If not, remember my warning.''*

Quigley heaved a sigh of relief as the apparitions faded from the room.

A cart drawn by two magnificent white horses entered the village. A blanket of snow covered the ground and in the distance the sound of the church bells were ringing merrily. A. Quigley Esquire, sat by the driver, his white hair stirred by the gentle breeze. His face had lost the pallor and the hardness was replaced by a smile. A servant from the hall walked by the side. His first stop was the home of Mrs. Meeson, Jack's wife, at the far end of the village. He knocked on the door and in a moment or two it was opened by a sad looking woman, a child of two years clutching her skirt.

''Yes''? she asked quietly.

Quigley struggled with his emotions at the sight of this poor woman and her child, and was at a loss for what to say to her. He held out his hand and took hers and held it.

''I..I er,'' he managed to say at last. *''I bring you glad tidings and wish you and your family a very happy Christmas.''*

''But, I don't under stand. Who are you?'' she asked.

''All will be revealed,'' he said.

Indicating to his servant by the wave of his hand. The servant and the driver took off the cart a large hamper and carried it to the cottage.

''May we be allowed to put it inside?'' asked Quigley.

Mrs. Meeson stepped aside to let them enter, and the hamper was placed on the hearth. Quigley opened it to reveal all manner of Christmas fare, a plucked goose, ham, pudding, toys for the children, and much more.

''I, still don't understand. Who are you? Why have you brought

all this...? '' she asked.

''You received a note I believe, to tell you to leave this cottage?''

''Yes.''

Quigley smiled. *''My dear, you can ignore that notice and live here rent free as long has you like and furthermore you will receive a pension from a fund to help you and your family to live.''*

A look of relief and joy came on her countenance.

''Sir,'' she managed to say at last, *''I thank you with all my heart. But I still don't know who you are.''*

Quigley walked to the door and opened it. *''My name,''* he said quietly, *''my name is Quigley, the owner of the colliery. Please, please try to forgive me for the wrong I have done.''*

Quigley sat alone on Christmas day it was late afternoon, and the room was in semi-darkness. A large fire burned in the grate the flames making shadows on the walls. He gazed at the flames as though fascinated. There was a smile on his face and in his hand a glass of port. A bible lay opened on the table beside him. Sounds of merriment from below in the servants quarters. A noise from the corner of the room interrupted his reverie, and he turned to see what it was. From out of the half light, moving slowly towards him were the three spirits of retribution.. Quigley, sat up in alarm. The glass of port fell from his hand to the floor.

''Oh why have you come? Why do you persecute me? Have I not done what you asked of me? Listen to the joy of my servants down below. Never before has this house rung with the sound of laughter, and I for the first time in my life feel a great happiness, for as the good book says: ***'It is more blessed to give than to receive'****. The spirit of Christmas is within me and will remain with me evermore.''*

''We have not come to persecute you, but to tell you that we are pleased. Enjoy the happiness of giving and caring and we will rest in peace.''

The apparitions faded and were gone. Quigley stood up and raised his arms.

''Thank you O Lord for my salvation,'' he cried. *''A happy, joyful Christmas to everyone.''*

Chapter 7

CHRISTMAS DAY IN THE WORKHOUSE.

To spend most of the day in perambulating the many wards which were to be found in the Stoke workhouse on Christmas Day in the year of 1888. The general public could have no conception of the magnitude of this great house and little knowledge of the idiosyncrasies of its inmates, the distress of families who through no fault of their own were compelled to seek refuge here which was regarded at that time, to be the largest poor-house in the county of Staffordshire.

The parish of Stoke at that time, comprised about two thirds of the Potteries district. Hanley, Longton, Fenton, Bucknall and even Bagnall. The population according to the 1881 census was 104,299.

The first workhouse was erected in Penkhull, but in 1883 a site known as the Spittals was purchased and a commodious building was erected. Over the years the property was extended to meet with the demand of admittances and the needs of the inmates which included a school to accommodate 250 scholars, a chapel for 400 to worship and a small hospital.

The master and matron were a Mr. and Mrs. Griffiths who had no easy task before them daily in visiting the different wards and administrating the running with the help of staff, this large institution. The area of land occupied by the various buildings was seven acres, it also had several acres of adjoining land for farming purposes which was worked by the young boy inmates, which provided the institution with nearly all its requirements. There was not one idle person who retains the use of his or her limbs. All have something to do and appear to do that willingly. Even the imbeciles in time learn to perform their allotted tasks with ease. About a dozen lads had mastered the mysteries of baking, plumbing and other skilled trades. The girls bake, cook, washing and ironing. The consumption of food was enormous. 50 sacks of flour per week were made into about four thousand loaves, meat averages about 2000 pounds, potatoes some 45 bushels. Three firkins of butter each week was contracted for.

THE DAILY ROUTINE.

The bell rang for the majority of inmates to rise at 5.45 a.m. Breakfast was provided an hour later, dinner was ready at mid-day, supper was eaten between 6 and 8 o'clock. For breakfast the inmates up to a certain age consisted of bread and milk gruel. The dinner varied from day to day, one day lobby, a few days of bread and cheese, the rest composed of suet and puddings sweetened with treacle. For supper, tea and bread and butter, occasionally cocoa. The principal outdoor work was farming mainly done by the boys. The gardens and walks were kept in order by the imbeciles. Most of the men were given the tasks of either stone breaking or opium picking, and this force was strengthened daily by wanderers and tramps.

Should there be any individual imagined that the life of a wanderer while a temporary sojourner in the Stoke workhouse had anything pleasant about it they were soon disenchanted. The number of casuals varied from 60 to 100 per week. Any person who applied for a nights shelter was detained for three days. On the first day he was called upon to break seven hundredweight of Clee Hill basalt stone. The stones must be broken to a given size, a grid being provided through which they must be pushed which will not admit any stone larger than 2.1/2 inches being passed through. For some, like the labourers and colliers the output of work was attained with ease but the majority who had not experienced hard labour were unable to reach their target were punished. Their food for this work was very generous. They were allowed 8 ounces of dry bread with cold water for breakfast and supper, and a piece of bread and cheese or broth and bread for their mid-day meal. They were provided with a deal board for their bed with a block of wood for a pillow.

FESTIVITIES.

The great dining hall with its lines of tables, the inmates all agog with anticipation for this was the one day they did not have to labour and have the joy of families being united. Whole families together for this one special day. It was Christmas Day. Mother, father and children all awaiting to have this one meal together. There was some of course that had no family and there were some that had seen better days.

There was one who was called Mary who it seemed had a fixation about her hair which she combed from early morning to late at night. It was a beautiful head of hair, white as carded wool.

Sally had been made to leave her bed on this day, much against her wishes for she had not left her bed voluntary for seven years. She was a stout lady, decidedly fat and certainly over forty. Her weight would be over fourteen stone. She laboured under the impression that her principle digestive organ contain no nourishing food but bones, and kept appealing for some medicine to remove them. She complained that she has no appetite, although she was masticating something all the time she spoke.

One of the oldest occupants of the house was an old lady who declared that she was ninety three years of age, and from what she said had once held a very high position in the Royal household and had been on intimate terms with Queen Victoria, and if credence was to be placed in her statements she must have been on intimate terms with her Majesty when she was a young girl, and probably was the only person in her station in life who could have boasted to have punished the queen for some mad girlish pranks. This old lady was probably an under servant at St. James's Palace during the reign of the previous King.

There was an old man who showed no anger if you doubted that he had passed the age of 109.

Another in the infirm ward who could speak most of the European languages, but admitted that he could never write them. He had been a considerable traveller in his day, and was a native of Polish Russia

It was no doubt on this special day, when the food served to the inmates was of a very high quality for a poor law institution. The first course was a vegetable soup the second, a plate of pork with potatoes and sprouts followed by Christmas pudding. Nearly all the ingredients of this dinner was produced and prepared on the premises. The remnants of the meal, which was hardly any, the dishes were taken away, and the master announced there would be a little entertainment.

There appeared on the improvised stage a lady, one of the inmates of the imbecile ward. She would be about forty years of age, the ravages of her malady and time now etched on a once pretty face. She curtsied and at once in a fine contralto voice *''Hark the Herald Angels sing.''* Unfortunately halfway through the second verse she stopped singing and looked around her in a bemused state. The master realising that she must have forgotten the lines joined in and raising his arms to the audience prompted them to join in. Within a few seconds the rafters rang with discordant sound. At the end of the carol the master with a smile on his face then appealed for quiet.

When order was restored he again raised his arms.

''I will'', he said. *''Now introduce you to a wonderful musician.''*

Soon this man made his appearance. Imagine if you will a man of medium height, broad shoulders, massive featured, and decidedly intellectual looking, who, in his workhouse clothing, for a moment might be mistaken for a skilled artisan, and you have an off-hand outline of:, *"THE PAGININI OF STOKE WORKHOUSE."*

''Where is your violin?'' the Master asked. *''Because I want you, if you will to give us a tune or two.''*

Without showing a slightest trace that anything was mentally wrong with him, the poor fellow made a graceful inclination of his head, said in a sharp, though decidedly musical undertone, ''With *pleasure,''* and he stepped smartly to the spot where the instrument was kept.

''Unfortunately I have only three strings on my violin, but I will do my best to gratify you.''

The choice of his first effort was left to him. He immediately tightened the strings and started to play with much spirit and perfect

"THE PAGININI OF STOKE WORKHOUSE."

accuracy, the "Men of Harlech", then "Home Sweet Home". It seemed that nothing could stop him except that when he was halfway through a piece by Lizt he paused for a few seconds taking down the violin from his chin and waving the bow at his spellbound audience.

''Ladies! Ladies! We really must not have so much talking!'' he remonstrated. Although you could have heard the proverbial pin drop during his recital.

This fine musician was found one day it appeared lying unconscious in a street in Hanley with his beloved instrument gripped in his hand, he was exhausted and starving and was taken to the Stoke Workhouse. When he recovered he could not remember his name or where he had come from, but he could remember that he was in Carl Rosa's orchestra, that he had led the bands at Bradford, Leeds and Halifax theatres, that he had composed much entr'acte music and had written several pieces, the names of which, with one exception, he could not call to mind. The piece he said was entitled *''The Bonny Bride of Lorne''* and was dedicated to the Marquis on the occasion of his marriage. He could play several instruments, the violin, viola, double bass, saxhorn, and cornet.

The master had left the platform and returned after a few minutes with a violin with the full compliment of strings and a composition for the violin by H.C.Blagrove. This took several minutes to play without the slightest hesitancy and with the greatest of ease. Every one was delighted with the mans skill, and doubtless wondered, at this very singular anomaly. The poor fellow was painfully polite, when the master promised him a new string. He had been at the Workhouse about twelve months, and his case had been more than once placed before the Stoke Guardians, and every effort had been made to try and find his origin but to no avail.
And so ended the times and Christmas Day in Stoke Workhouse in the year 1888.

The Workhouse in the area known as The Spittalls was later made into a large hospital, and known today as The City General.

Chapter 8
A PRAYER FOR CHRISTMAS.

The headline on the 23rd. December 1938 in the local newspaper in bold black type read:-

**HOPE IS RUNNING OUT
FOR THE TRAPPED MEN.**

It as now been three days since the rock fall entombed three miners', and reports from the pit head this morning gave little hope that they are still alive. But, said the spokesman, every effort is being made to reach them, with teams working round the clock. The three miners are:-Jack Thomas, aged 30, Collier. Married with one daughter. Harry Williams, aged 23, Loader. Single. Thomas Rowley, aged 14 Haulage hand, Harry Williams was to be married at Christmas to his childhood sweetheart Anne Grainger. Relatives and friends of Miss Grainger have tried to persuade her to leave the Pit head where she has been since Tuesday in a state of shock. For nearly three days she has remained, indifferent to the inclement weather awaiting for the news that her loved one would soon be rescued. She now seems to be in a state of torpidity, muttering at times incoherently, and sometimes through the anguish a pitiful cry of: "*I want my Harry. Please, please take me to him.*" On several occasions she has had to be restrained from trying to gain access to the cage. Doctor Robinson who has been at the scene since yesterday, is very concerned for her health and has suggested that she must be removed, and forcibly if need be.

Three thousand feet below the surface and some three miles inbye and behind tons of rock, the three miners' squat in this tomb, exhausted by the effort of moving and ridding the rock to try and escape. The want of sustenance, food and water is beginning to tell. The lights of their oil lamps have been turned very low to conserve the precious oil, knowing as they do that in a short time they will be in total darkness.

The air is becoming stale, this they know will not last many more hours. Harry laboriously rose to his feet and moved to the fall of rock. With some effort he took up in his raw and bleeding hands a large piece and threw it behind him.

"*Wot tryin' ter do 'Arry?*" asked Jack.

Harry turned with anger in his eyes. "*Wot the 'ell dust think ah'm doin'? Ah conna sit 'ere doin' nite.*"

"*Look mate ah've towd thee, it's useless. O' they't doin is usin' up air. Wey o want ter get ite. Thee anna forgot us thee'll be through any tarme. So sit thee sel dine,*" said Jack.

Harry reluctantly did as he was told. "*Ah've got ter bey ite Jack, thee knowst ah've promised ter wed Anne on Christmas Eve*" he said softly. "*I wonder wot dee it is, it inna Christmas Eve is it Jack?*"

"*No, not yet. Dunna fret youth, thee'll 'ave us ite in tarme mark me words,*" Jack replied.

"*Ah promised ah Ken, eh's me little brother, ter tak 'im up McIlroys, th' big shop up 'Anley ter see Santa,*" said Tommy.

"*Good lad.*" Said Jack. "*Dust believe in Santa?*"

"*Na,*" replied Tommy. "*But ah young un does, eh's only five.*"

"*Ah remember wen ah were a lad a bit younger than you Tommy, it were abite ninetane twenty two. Me faither tuk us young uns, me two brothers and little sister ter Stoke Station ter see Santa arrive be train. Lord Mayor were theer and hundreds o' folk. Thee wer a an army band pleein' an 'e got into an open coach pulled by two jet black 'osses wi' wate plumes on their yeds. Thee set off fer 'Anley wi' thray men in front carryin' a banner wi' th' words 'Santa Claus is coming after us to Mcilroy's. Wey o' follered 'im ter 'Anley weer 'undreds o' folk wer weetin'. Ah've never sain a site lark it, ah an never will agen ah dunner serpose.*"

"*Did yer ever tak your little girl ter see Santa Jack?*" Tommy asked.

"*Oh ah, ah took 'er last year, it wer a tanner ter sey 'im in 'is grotto an 'e gave 'er a little toy. Ah've promised ter tak 'er this year an o',* " replied Jack.

"*D'yer like Christmas Jack?*" asked Tommy.

"*Like Christmas lad? Cus ah do. It's magical, mysterious lark. An' o' course an 'e wer born, Jesus Christ, the son o' God*"

"*Ah know Jesus wer born, But wots mean- magical?*" asked Tommy.

"*Well it's different from other tarmes o' th' year. Folk wishin' yer well a feelin o' good will an most o' o----*"

"*Shush!*" *Shush!*" Harry exclaimed jumping to his feet. "*Did yer 'ear it?*"

"*Wot?*" asked Jack.

"*Knockin!*"

Silence reigned for several moments, ears strained.

"*Theyt 'earin' things,*" remarked Jack.

"*Ah tell thee ah 'eard knockin'* ."

"*Well ah didna. Didst they Tommy?*"

"Na."

"*Well yo wunner would yer, blabberin' on abite Christmas. Christ inna 'elpin us is 'e? A dog shudner die lark this--Christ!*"

Harry sat down, put his head in his arms and started to sob.

At that moment one of the lamps flickered and went out. An eerie silence ensued broken only by an occasional creaking of the remaining timbers supporting the roof.

"*Ah think*", said Jack quietly, "*ah think lads it's tarme wey said a little prayer*"..... "*O God, give us, young Tommy, Harry and me, strength and courage to face the next few 'ours in this terrible place, and if thy will be done, I beseech thee to give comfort to our families that will be left up above for the sake of your son Jesus Christ. O Saviour, Lord, to thee we pray, Whose love has kept us safe, protect us through the coming hours, and ever save us by Thy powers, Be with us now, in mercy nigh and spare Thy servants when they cry; Forgive our sins, and receive our prayers, Thy light throughout our darkness give*..........." "*I can remember some of the 23 Psalm... Yea though I walk through the valley of the shadow of death, I will fear no evil.*

For Thou art with me; Thy rod and Thy staff comfort me. Amen''.

The second lamp flickered and died and they were left in almost complete blackness. Harry felt young Tommy's hand in his and he put his arm around him and drew him close.

"ah think lads it's tarme wey said a little prayer"

''*Jack?*'' asked Tommy in a quiet voice.

''*Wot son?*''

''*Wot did yer mean wen yer said that Christmas was magic?*''

''*Well, thees a lot a things that 'appen. Thees a part of a poem ah remember that tells some o' the magic o' th' country...*''

"Have you seen by any chance,
The moonbeams an' th' fairies dance,
Beautiful pearls made out of dew,
Flimsy, like gossamer, the spider too
Spins a web for all to see
And wonder at its intricacy.

Christmas sometimes brings snow to the ground,
A white mantle silencing all the sound.
Tell tale marks reveal the fox,
A rabbit, a weasel, scampers o'er the rocks.
The vixen coughs, the robin sings,
On Christmas eve the church bell rings,
Calling the people for congregation,
To give thanks for their salvation."

''*That's magic Jack,*'' whispered Tommy.

''*Ah lad thees a lot more, things wey dunna appreciate until its too late*''.

''*Didyer 'ear that, that knockin'? Theer it is agen!*'' exclaimed Harry jumping to his feet and stumbling panic stricken to the fall.

''*Ah, ah did.*'' shouted Harry rising to his feet.

''*An' mey.*'' shouted Tommy.

The knocking was louder now, and the three answered by shouting.

''*Ello,*'' came the voice from beyond. ''*Wey'll bey with you soon.*''

The three turned and faced each other smiling and then embraced.

''*Thank God,*'' said Jack

''*Ah,*'' said Harry,

"It's Magic," said Tommy *"An' thee Christmas prayer Jack."*

The flame in the last remaining lamp slowly died and they were enveloped in blackness. Their embrace became much tighter.

"Dunna worry lads it wunna bey long." Jack said.

They stepped from the cage, it was dark and it was snowing. The sky was clear and the stars shone brightly. In the distance the church bells peeled merrily. It was Christmas Eve. Young Tommy looked up at Jack smiling.

"It's magic Jack."

"Ah lad," the collier replied, *"and it's Christmas."*

Anne, her long vigil over, clung to her man sobbing hysterically.

"Thank God," she cried.

Chapter 9
THE CONVERSION

Tummy (Tommy) Thompson was a hard man, a drunkard, a wife beater who was not averse in the ill treatment of his children, of which he was the father of three. Two sons and a daughter. The two eldest had left the home early to avoid the cruel beatings. Mary the eldest, was married at eighteen, and Harry the eldest lad had enlisted in the army when he was seventeen and a half, leaving the youngest, Tommy aged eleven. Tommy had been named after his father when Tummy was in a rare benevolent mood.

Tummy was a puddler and worked at Shelton Bar. The work was hot and dangerous. To replace the fluid he lost in sweat, he avidly drank with great pleasure, gallons of beer. It was the Saturday before Christmas. Christmas Day would be on the following Tuesday. Tummy had received a good pay out, known locally as 'Bull Week', and with a small savings, which he had contributed to each week, he was flushed, and all seemed well with his world. By dinner time he had drunk his fill and returned home to satisfy his other hunger. He withdrew a large bottle of ale from his jacket pocket, and placed it on the table. His mood was not angry but sombre.

''Wees me dinner?'' he demanded.

Sally, his wife, moved quickly to the back kitchen and returned within a few moments with a steaming bowl of lobby and placed it before him at the same time giving him a spoon. Taking up a knife she started to slice pieces of bread.

''Do way o' wees after 'ave lobby, is there nowt else woman?'' he asked.

Young Tommy sat on the settle and watched his father with fear in his eyes, and he wondered if he was going to be violent again.

''Ah said, dunna way 'ave nowt else in the 'ouse but lobby. Wot's up woman ah yer deaf?''

Sally gave him a scathing look still holding the bread knife in her hands.

''No. Way dunna 'ave ite else!'' she shouted back at him

''And dust know way thee inna ite else?''

''Nar. Tell us!''

He took up a slice of bread and pulling it to pieces dropped them into the bowl. He looked up at her with menace in his eyes.

''Because ah've never got any money 'ave ah?'' she answered, her voice rising to a shrill scream.

''Dunna they scream at may woman. Or yer'll bay feelin' this!''

He scowled at her showing her his clenched fist. He held her stare for several seconds, daring her to reply before continuing with his meal. No more words were spoken, the silence broken only by the intake of food from his spoon. Soon the lobby was eaten and with the passing of wind, he replaced the spoon and reached for the bottle of ale pouring himself a mug full.

There was a knock on the door.

''Goo on, sey 'oo it is'', he indicated to the lad with an impatient movement of his hand.

Young Tommy moved quickly and returned in a moment or two.

''It's the vicar,'' he said quietly and with some apprehension.

''Wot's 'e want?''

'' 'E says 'e wants a word with you.''

His father's eyes opened wide. *''Wi may?''* he asked.

Young Tommy nodded.

''Wot's eh want wi' may. Ast they bin up ter some mischief at that choir?''

''No Dad.''

''Ah'll 'ave the skin off thee back if thee ast. Dust 'ear me?''

Tummy poured himself another drink.

''Yer'd best tell 'im ter come in,'' he said at last.

Tommy turned and left the room returning a few moments later with the vicar. He was tall and angular, with a large Adam's apple bobbing up and down within an oversized clerical collar. He nodded at Tummy.

''Ggood afternoon Mr. Thompson. I trust you are well?''

Tummy nodded in return, *''Ah well enough. Wot can ah do fer yo?''*

The rude and abrupt answer put the vicar ill at ease, for Tummy's reputation as a bully was known even in ecclesiastical circles.

''Wwwell,'' he stuttered. *''I've cccome to see if you wwwill be attending evensong tomorrow evening?''*

Tummy had just started to swallow a drink of beer, and the question made the mechanism in his throat go haywire, and he started to choke uncontrollably and the beer that still remained in his mouth sprayed out catching the poor vicar full in the face. Sally's immediate reaction was to put her hands to her face to try and hide from the shame, then quickly she rose and with the front of her pinafore outstretched in her hands, proceeded to wipe the offending beer from the vicar's face. Tummy, after several attempts to clear his throat, took another drink.

''Wot didst see?'' he asked putting the mug down on the table.

The Vicar thanked Sally for attempting to dry his face and pulling out an handkerchief from his pocket finished the task.

''Ah said!'' Tummy asked again, *''Wot didst see''*?

Sally turned from the vicar and faced her husband with a scathing look.

''Dunna see yer sorry, will yer?'' she demanded.

Tummy took another drink from his mug.

''Ah wanna tokin' ter yo was ah eh?''

The vicar returned the handkerchief to his pocket then held out his hands in an attempt to pacify the stormy scene which was about to erupt at any moment.

''Please Mister and Missus Thompson do not distress yourselves!''

Sally left the room muttering incoherently to herself.

''I said, wwwould you bbbe attending Evensong tomorrow evening?''

''Wot's mane, mey goo ter church termorrer naight. Mey?'' Asked Tummy, with a funny bewildered, astounded look on his face.

''Yyes'' replied the vicar.

''Wot fer?''

''It's a special service. The last Sunday before Christmas. Advent you know. Young Tommy here is playing a very important part''

'' 'E is 'is 'e. Wot's 'e doin' then?''

''Tommy has a very fine voice as you may know.''

'' 'E 'as as'e?'' Tummy took another drink and burped.

''So, wot's that got ter do wi' me gooin ter church?'' he asked.

The vicar started to wring his hands and noticed how clammy they were, and at this moment in time wished that he had volunteered for overseas missionary work.

''Wwwell young Tom will be singing solo and I thought, wwell I'er thought that you would er...being his father er... would like to tttake the opportunity to er... hear him sing.''

Tummy took another drink out of the mug and drained it. He looked first of all into the mug, then turned his attention to the poor cleric sitting uncomfortably on the settle. A few seconds went by, which to the poor man seemed hours, and he seemed to wither with every one. Sally returned giving a reassuring smile to the vicar and a scathing look at her hateful husband.

''Way'll say.'' Tummy said at last taking the bottle of beer off the table and filled his mug and, thrusting the bottle towards the vicar, he asked, with a vestage of a smile on his face, *''Would yer care fer a swaller''*?

''Nno, no thank you,'' the vicar replied and quickly rose to his feet. *''I must be going, but I do hope to see you tomorrow evening.''* He gave a little bow to Sally and a smile and was gone.

''Yo're wicked yo' are! Wicked! Treating the poor mon lark

that!'' She stood over him almost daring him to strike her. Her hands on her hips a look of defiance on her face.

''It justs shows 'ow yer were brote up! Brote up! Dragged up more lark it! Wot will that mon think of us? That poor mon! And ma lad theer.'' She paused and turned to the boy sitting on the settle. ''That *lad, that poor lad. 'E 'll never bay able ter 'owd 'is 'ead up in that church agen''.*

The memory of what had just transpired was just to much for her and she broke down and started to cry. Tummy threatened to rise from his chair.

''Shut yer face woman or ah'll shut it fer yer!''

She thrust her tear stained face near to his.

''Goo on then! Goo on then! 'It me! That's o' yer fit fer, drink and 'ittin' women an' kids! Goo on then 'it me!'' Sally screamed at him.

With the back of his hand he struck her across the face and floored her. Young Tommy quickly bent down beside her to comfort and protect her from further blows.

''Leave me mam alone.'' he shouted at him.

Tummy picked up his mug drained it, burped and smiled satanically. The Sunday evening tea was sparse and was dispensed with quickly. Young Tommy and his mother were dressed and ready for church, waiting patiently and watching with some apprehension, Tummy wrestling with a stiff white collar, and a black tie. His face was the hue of reddish purple, his eyes sticking out like chapel hat pegs. Sally at times, thought he was having some kind of fit, such were his antics.

''Way th' 'ell people 'ave ter wear such soddin' things, ah'll never know!'' he exclaimed, pausing to rest his arms. *'''Ow long ah yer gooin ter bey mon, we're gooin ter be late! Con yer not 'ear the church bell ringing?''* she asked with a tone of anxiety and urgency in her voice.

He turned to her in anger, half the collar fastened to the collar stud the other half waving about his ear hole and the tie hanging loose about his neck like a hangman's noose.

"Shut it!" he shouted at her, and turned once again to face the mirror hanging over the mantelpiece and the struggle started all over again until, in desperation, he snatched the offending accessories from his neck and threw them into the fire.

"Sod it! Sod it!" he exclaimed violently, his whole being now consumed in uncontrollable anger. He turned at last to young Tommy who was sitting on the settle, half afraid yet half amused at his father's antics.

"Yo!" Tummy shouted. *"Goo and fetch me muffler from the back o' the parlour dooer."*

"Yo anna gooin ter church in thee muffler?" Sally asked.

He faced her with violence in his eyes. *"It's either that or ah dunna goo at o'!"*

The lad handed him the scarf and he snatched it from him and tied it around his neck. He looked at himself in the mirror approvingly.

"Ah that's better." he said, calmer and a little happier. *"Raight let's goo"*

He took up his cap from the hook behind the parlour door and without any further ado placed it on his head. Passing Fred Hall's the undertaker's, he noticed that the Antelope public house situated next door on the corner of Marsh street and Trinity Street, was just about to open its doors. The bell at the Holy Trinity Church, Next door but one, in Trinity street, was tolling much faster now, urging the stragglers to be quick as the service was about to begin.

"Ah'm just gooin 'in 'ere fer a quick un. Yo goo on ah'll say yer inside" Tummy said as he opened the pub door.

"Yo anna got time ter...."

Before she could finish the sentence he had vanished behind the hostelry door. Evensong had been in progress about ten minutes or more when the Church door opened and then closed with a terrific bang. The sound of steel tipped boots mingled with the squeak of leather echoed in the church. Heads turned, necks craned and the vicar halted in his utterings to see who was responsible for the desecration.

Tummy spied Sally halfway down on the left hand side, and hurried to the pew, the tempo of the noise increasing. On entering the pew, his right foot caught in the side, and he tripped, landing on top of an irate spinster who screamed in alarm. So unaccustomed was she to have a rough oaf on top of her smelling of beer, and certainly not in the sanctity of church. Tummy extricated himself with difficulty, and sat down beside his wife. The shame on her face was evident and she tried in vain to ignore him. The service had now ceased altogether, the vicar endeavouring with a series of coughs to resume. He held out his arms like a salvationist and raised his voice: -

"But there was no room at the inn and no room to sleep except in the stable. That night the Baby was born."

He paused and looked at his congregation and seeing that order had been restored he proceeded, in a much quieter voice, to tell the story of the Nativity.

"In the fields outside Bethlehem the shepherds were guarding their sheep, when a light suddenly shone around them and an angel called: ``I bring you good tidings of great joy which shall be to all people. For unto you this day in the City of David a Saviour, which is Christ the Lord.`` "

The organ started to play and a voice, pure and crystal clear, started to sing:- *"Glory to God in the highest and on earth goodwill toward men........ "*

The dulcet tones continued no other sound could be heard and minutes of sanctity prevailed as never before. Tears welled in Sally's eyes and she looked at the man sitting next to her. He sat, cap in hand, staring from whence the Angelic voice came, his eyes not blinking and his face had attained a softness that she had never seen before. All through the service he never moved but just sat and stared. Sally was getting worried now and wished the service would end quickly, even though it would mean the end of her boy singing, for she was sure now that something unreal had happened to this wretch she called her husband. At last the service ended and the choir, led by Tommy singing: *"O Lamb of God that taketh away the sins of the world,"* filed slowly down the aisle to the vestry. The church emptied and many wondered why the strange rough man never moved and the woman by his side was crying. After awhile she shook him. But he still stared into space and did not move.

"Tummy, wot is the matter? Speak ter me mon!" She got to her feet and put her hands on his shoulders.

"Tummy! Tummy! speak ter me can't yer?"

The vicar on his way to his vestry to unrobe, witnessed the drama taking place and asked if he could be of some assistance.

"Some'its 'appened ter me 'usband!" she said softly through the tears. "Ah *think,* " she started to sob. *"Ah think eh's 'ad a stroke."*

The vicar knelt down beside him and looked with suspicion in Tummy's eyes and smelling the beer on his breath remembered the day before when this wretch, this man, had behaved abominably towards him and even tried to ruin this Evensong.

"Are you sure he's not drunk?"

Sally was taken back by the man's unfeeling. She straightened up and looked the vicar in the eyes.

"Drunk! 'ow dare yer say eh's drunk, an yo' a vicar! Ah ought ter know if 'e's drunk or not ah've sane 'im drunk enough tarmes!" she exclaimed with anger in her voice. *"Ah tell yer 'e's 'ad a stroke 'e 'as an' wants a doctor."*

The vicar got to his feet and started to wring his hands.

"Dear me! Dear me! What shall I do?"

The poor man had not been trained at the university for this type of emergency and in church of all places. Young Tommy had now joined them. He first looked at his mother then at the vicar, then knelt down in front of his father, took his large work gnarled hands in his, and looked into his eyes.

"Dad, Dad", he said softly. *"What's the matter?"*

He felt his father's hands tighten on his then a flicker of the eyebrows. A tear ran from the corner of one eye, then another. His mouth opened slowly and the voice, dry, rasping trying to make words. At last the noise became coherent.

"Dad, Dad", he said softly. *"What's the matter?"*

"Tommy, Tommy, ah've seen Him." A spate of tears ran down his face.

"Seen who Dad?" asked Tommy, feeling a strangeness come over him because never in his entire life, felt or been so close to him.

Tummy pulled the boy close to his chest and at the same time took Sally's hand in one of his.

"Ah've seen," he muttered, looking up through his tears first at Sally then at the Vicar *"Ah've seen the face of God,"* he said softly and with reverence.

He then held them both in his stare for a moment or two, but neither spoke, made speechless by the statement he had made.

''And ah 'eard His voice when you were singing lad such a beautiful voice. Con yer fergive me?''

He started to cry as though his very heart would break. With her other hand Sally stroked his head then bent down and kissed his forehead. How many years had passed since she had done that she could not remember. She felt strange; like a new courtship a new beginning.

''C'mon Tummy lad let's go 'ome''

The trio rose and walked down the aisle hand in hand and left the church. The next day was Christmas Eve. Tummy had risen early and made ready, the fire was lit and the breakfast, though sparse, was made. He was a different person. He had lost the hard selfish expression and his countenance seem to beam a goodliness they, his family had never seen before.

When they had dined he looked at his wife and son and said: *''We are now goin'ter 'Anley town ter buy the things ter celebrate Christmas. Ah've a bit o' money saved and yer con 'ave anything yer want,''* he paused and smiled, *''within reason o'course and then we'll go and see our Mary and me little grandson ah've never seen, and we'll invite 'em 'ere fer Christmas Dee.''*

He looked up at the ceiling, still smiling his eyes gleaming bright. *''O Lord I thank thee,''* he said quietly and with reverence.

Chapter 10

THE PUB CRAWL.

It was the Eve before Christmas in the Brook Inn that was situated in Sydney Street in Hanley, in the year of 1934.
The bar was crowded with colliers, potters and forgemen.

Joe Derricot and Jack Thomas were well down their third pint enjoying in their way the festivities of Yule tide.
A feeling of goodwill prevailed, even the aroma of a cheap cigar pervaded the room. The clatter of dominoes from one table and the distinct murmur of fifteen to two and one for his "wotsit" came from another table as four of the men were playing cribbage. A discordant sound of a piano with the women singing a carol came from the Smoke room.

"*Ah lark Christmas dust they Jack?* " asked Joe.

"*Ah do,*" replied Jack. "*It's the one tarme in th' year when yer con forget th' pit fer a few days and get a bellyful o' ale an' enjoy yersel.*"

"*At 'avin another?*" asked Joe, lifting his mug to drain it.

"*Ah*" replied Jack, "*Ah'll 'ave another before closin'. Did yer 'ear about Tummy Jones on coal face tother dee boastin' abite 'ow much ale eh could sup in one nate?*"

"*No*", replied Joe, paying for the two pints and taking another drink. "*And 'ow much did Tummy reckon eh could drink?.*"

"*Well thee wer a bet that eh cudna goo ter o' the pubs in 'Anley and drink a pint in every one.*"

"*Ah, and did 'e?*"

Jack took a drink and lowered the glass on the bar. A smile appeared on his countenance.

"*Na. Eh did abite sixteen*" His smile broadened and he started to laugh. "*Thee funt 'im iteside th' Crown an' Anchor in th' gutter*

eh cudna goo ter o' the pubs in 'Anley and drink a pint in every one

singing 'is yed off.'' He started to laugh louder now hardly able to talk.

''Wot 'appened?'' asked Joe.

'' Bobby's come,... two on 'em...eh 'ad goo at em.''

''Wot's mean, fatin?''

''Ah then thee dragged 'im awee and took 'im ter th' cop shop.''

''Mind yer, eh didner do ser bad it would take some doin' ter drink a pint in every pub in 'Anley'', remarked Joe taking a long drink from his glass. *''But ah think ah could do it.''*

''Oo they?'' queried Jack.

''Ah mey. Wouldst lark a bet on it?''

''Ah 'ere's ten bob, says they costna do it,'' said Jack putting a ten shilling note on the bar.

''Do any of yo lot want ter 'ave a bet?'' Jack shouted to the other men in the bar.

''Wot's the bet?'' they asked.

"Eh says, Joe 'ere, says eh con drink a pint in every pub in 'Anley. Ten bob says eh conna. If eh wins eh taks the ten bobs if eh loses eh pays us"

"Dust know 'ow maypubs thee are in 'Anley Joe?" asked Jim, a potter.

"Yes, I know what ah'm doin', an 'im 'ere con come wi' me, if eh wants ter prove it" said Joe.

"Ah'll come," said Jack, *"But ah anna drinkin' a pint wi' they"*

About six of the men in the bar gave their ten shillings to the barman to hold.

"When is it ter be?" asked one.

"Boxing Dee nate," said Joe *"Wey'll start suppin' in Little Borough, and finish if o' goos well in th' Bush."*

"Ah, that's weer yo will finish up, in a bush flat on thee back," remarked a collier laughing.

Albion Square, Hanley.
Waggon and Horses Pub

The following ode so cleverly composed by Pauline Shufflebotham portrays the progress of the pub crawl.

A PUB CRAWL IN HANLEY IN DAYS OF OLD.

In this tiny Little Borough, surrounding Market Square,
Everyone was happy, everyone was doing fine.
You could get a good drink in the Albion
Munroes or The Tontine.

The Marquis of Granby arrived here in style
In a Waggon and Horses of unusual design
Fronted by a Black Lion and a Unicorn
Decked with gold to make it shine.

He'd travelled all the length of the Globe
He was tired and hungry... 'Twas the end of the line,
So he rested and dined at the Grand Hotel.
And from a Golden Cup he drank some Wine.

He went to the Market Tavern,
Then the Sea Lion to search for a wren,
Then onto the George and Dragon
For a good game of darts with the men.

Now he fancied his chances at cribbage
So he looked for a gambling den.
He discovered the Burton Stores
I was related to the landlord me sen!

He followed the form of the racing,
Lost all his money in the "Old Pig Pen".
How could he have been such a silly old fool
Still I suppose it would happen again!

He continued his tour of Hanley
In the Bulls Head pub that night.
He met the Duke of Wellington
With a lass of sheer delight.

He tried to take her from him
But got into a fight.
It seems he made some comment
Then argued black was white.

Now while the two were rowing
And punching with all their might.
Up from Stoke with Three Crowns on his head,
The Prince of Wales came into sight.

Mounted on a Black Horse
With his armour shining bright
He whisked her off into the sunset
Didn't that just serve them right!!

Then Shangai Lil arrived in town,
Bewildered she ran into the Coachmaker's Arms.
He fed her Grapes from off the Vine
And she fell victim to all his charms.

Meanwhile at the Port Vale Inn
Man met woman without any qualms
If you ask me what was going on
All I can say is... they weren't singing psalms!!

The piano was playing in the Elephant and Castle,
As closing time was nigh.
Then as the Angel blew her trumpet,
The Star lit up the sky.

The Welsh man played upon his Harp,
Glory to God on High.
But when the French man played upon his Horn
Go home...Was the landlord's cry!!

As the Dewdrop fell on Bluebell woods
There was trouble at a tavern called the Mill
Then we heard the sound of a Ring o' Bells
From a church o'er the hill.

The Sun came up it was finally dawn,
But the ale was flowing still.
I don't understand what attracted them so
I guess I never will.

The Highland Laddie had a shocking time
with his mates at the old Queens Head
When he glanced at the clock over the "Electric Bar
He remembered what he had previously said.

He had made a promise not to be late,
To the girl he had recently wed.
But alas he was persuaded to have one more pint
What a shame he was so easily led!

When he arrived home, it was just coming light,
So he tried to sneak up the stairs to bed.
Quiet as a Lamb to the top he crept
But he was met by his wife instead!

Where have you been again she scorned
Then she began to frown.
He said "Don't get angry sweetest one,
I've only been with the Mechanics in town"

Suddenly he felt a thud
Like Three Tuns come tumbling down,
She landed him a heavy blow
Like lead upon his Crown.

This knocked him now at last to sleep,
Neath the eiderdown
He was seeing double,
As at last he hit the sack.

He dreamt he was a Woodman
His name was Timber Jack.
Just in Time he reached the forest
Out of breath.. To see a pack

Of Antelopes, running puff, puff, puff,
Across the Railway track,
With a Golden Lion in hot pursuit,
No courage did he lack.

For a Bird in Hand is worth two in the Bush,
And there ain't no turning back.
Then Jack awoke with such a start
To more unrelenting flack.

So the moral of this story boys
I am about to reveal.
If she's annoyed at what you have done,
And her nagging seems unreal.

If your ego's been damaged by what she has said,
And you've really been taken to heel.
Don't say one thing, then do another,
Just think now and then how she'll feel.

Though I could go on for many awhile
To let the truth unfold.
These are my recollections,
There's lots more still untold.

Things have changed in many ways
But in my heart I hold,
My memories of the Market Square
And Hanley's pubs of old.

Joe managed to win the bet, but what a price he had to pay. It was fortunate that he had with him Jack his mate who, with difficulty got him home to his wife who berated him without mercy. Now in his eightieth year he often boasts of the Christmas when he drank a pint of beer in every pub in Hanley.

The good thing you may say, is that Joe never touched another drop from that day to this.

Chapter 11

THE HEALING.

It was nice to go shopping with your daughter, Mrs. Martin thought, an elderly lady who had reached her allotted span.

The town was crowded and coming from a quiet country village she became a bit overwhelmed but nevertheless she was happy, regarding the day as a treat.

Although Christmas was a few months away she thought she would take this opportunity to get some of the gifts for her children and friends.

''Are you alright mother?'' her daughter Helen asked. *''You look a little confused. Would you like to go home now?''*

''No, my dear, I'm fine,'' she answered.

''Well you will let me know when you want to go home, wont you?''

''Of course I will,'' her mother said. *''We'll just go to that big store in the market square I want to buy a cardigan for your father.''*

Reaching the Market Square she tripped and fell.

''Mother!'' Helen shouted in alarm, stooping down to try and assist her. *''Are you alright, let me try and get you on your feet.''*

Mrs. Martin with effort raised herself to a sitting position, the distress showed plainly on her now pale face.

''No, leave me a few seconds, I'll be alright directly, the fall has left me feeling sickly,'' she said quietly.

By this time a crowd had gathered all looking at the elderly lady with compassion.

''Can I help?'' asked one man. *''Do you want me to get an ambulance, she looks rather poorly.''*

''I, I don't know,'' replied Helen. *''How do yo feel now mother, can we get you to your feet?''*

''I don't think I can, I can't move my leg and I am in a lot of

pain''.

''Do you mind if I have a look, I do first aid in the pit,'' said the man.

''Please. I would be grateful.''

The man bent down and could see at once a distinct swelling in the upper part of the leg.

''Try and move your foot'', he asked Mrs. Martin.

''I can't. It's very painful.''

The man felt the area tenderly with his hands.

''I'm afraid it looks like a fractured femur,'' he said, looking with concern at Mrs. Martin then at Helen. *''We'd better get an ambulance.''*

....

''I'm afraid,'' the nurse said addressing Helen who was sitting in the waiting room of the infirmary. *''Your mother has broken her leg and is rather poorly, it will be the shock you know, so we have admitted her for a few days''.*

''Can I go and see her?'' asked Helen.

''Of course, but don't stay to long, we've sedated her because of the pain, she may be asleep. So, please do not disturb her.''

In the weeks that followed, with the removal of the plaster and physiotherapy, Mrs. Martin with the aid of a stick, walked slowly about trying to do the womanly tasks. Her face was now etched with constant pain and sleepless nights.

''Oh, Helen why, why am I in so much pain? I cant sleep, I am trying so hard to walk but the pain is unbearable at times.''

She lowered her head on her breast and started to sob.

Helen her daughter full of compassion for her mother put her arm around her to console her.

''What does the doctor say?'' Helen asked.

''He says in time it will get better, be patient, at your age bones and tissues take a long time to heal. But Helen it's four months now

since I fell, surely I should be better by now. The pain seems to be getting worse, I can't stand much more.''

''Has the doctor given you any tablets for the pain?'' Helen asked.

''Yes, but I still don't get any relief. Night and day, nag, nagging pain all the time, I cant go on Helen, I cant bear it much longer.''

Helen with her husband arrived at her parents house on Christmas morning with presents for her mother and father.

''A happy Christmas to you both,'' she said kissing them both and handing them their presents. *''How are you today Mother, a lot better I hope?''*

''No dear, I'm no better,'' she answered the pain evident in her eyes.

''I am taking her to see a specialist after Christmas. She can't go on like this.'' Mr. Martin remarked.

''Helen!''

''Yes mother?''

''Would you take me to church?''

''But mother, will you be able to manage? It's snowing.''

''Please,'' she implored *''I really must go, please.''*

Helen looked at her father for support.

''Alright,'' he said *''If you must, we'll all go.''*

''Thank you.'' Mrs. Martin uttered.

It was a slow and painful journey to the village church, a good inch of snow covered the ground. On entering the church, she indicated that for some reason unknown to herself, she wanted first to go into the church annexe which was used for various functions, and the Sunday school.

On one wall there were drawings portraying parables of the bible done by the pupils in crayon.

Mrs. Martin looked at them, and at one she became transfixed and in a few moments tears welled in her eyes, and she started to cry.

"If only, If only, I was able to touch his robe."

"Mother please don't cry," pleaded Helen.

The picture was of Jesus with a flowing robe, and a woman immediately behind him touching the hem of his garment.

The text read:

The woman touched His garment and was healed.

"If only", she uttered, and with the help of her daughter and husband walked slowly into the church.

The service, being Christmas Day was mainly about the story of the Nativity. Helen glanced at her mother sitting beside her. Her eyes were closed and looked to be in some kind of trance, or in fervent prayer, at times her lips moved. Helen was concerned for her, and took her hand in hers, it was cold but made no movement. Should she, Helen thought, arouse her from this trance like state, or wait until the end of the service. She looked again at her mother's face, her breathing seemed normal and her colour was the same. She decided to wait.

"The lesson is taken from St. Luke Chapter 8.43-48."

Oulton Church

> *And a woman having an issue of blood twelve years, which had spent all her living upon physicians, neither could be healed of any. Came behind Him and touched the border of his garment; and immediately her issue of blood staunched. And Jesus said, "Who touched me?" When all denied, Peter and they that were with Him said, Master, the multitude throng Thee and press Thee, and sayeth thou, Who touched me? And Jesus said, "Somebody hath touched me; for I perceive that virtue is gone out of me". And when the woman saw that she was not hid, she came trembling, and falling down before Him, she declared unto Him before all the people for what cause she had touched Him, and how she was healed immediately. And He said unto her, "Daughter, be of good comfort; thy faith hath made thee whole; go in peace."*

Slowly the congregation departed from the church, but the Martin family still sat in their pew.

''*Wake her!*'' Mr. Martin urged Helen.

Helen, still holding her mother's hand, now shook it.

''*Mother, Mother,*'' she said quietly.

Mrs. Martin's eyes flickered then opened wide and stared intently at the lectern.

''*Has he gone?*'' she asked.

''*Who?*''

''*The man in the long robe who read the lesson,*'' she replied rather impatiently.

''*But mother, Mr. Puxley the church warden read the lesson about the Nativity, and he wore a suit not a robe.*'' Helen replied.

''*No! No!*'' Mrs. Martin exclaimed. ''*I tell you it was a man in a long robe and he read the parable about the healing from St. Luke. You know like the children's drawing in the church room. I saw him clearly. Don't you believe me?*''

''*Yes mother if you say so. Shall we go home?*

They rose from the pew and into the aisle.

''*Helen,*'' Mrs. Martin halted, a smile on her face, her eyes gleamed brightly, ''*Helen I am free from pain. I have been healed.*''

Chapter 12
HE THAT IS WITHOUT SIN.

"But the boy didn't do it!" exclaimed Mrs. Whalley. *"He was at school all day!"*
The police sergeant smiled. *"So that's what he told you?"*

"Yes and I believe him. My boy is not a thief, nor is he a liar."

"Would you believe me if I told you that he had not been to school for two days?" said the sergeant.

Mrs. Whalley's eyes opened wide and her mouth opened in surprise. Her hand trembling, sought the door frame to support her. Her face was deathly pale.

"Are you all right missus, is your husband in?" asked the policeman.

"No," she answered, her voice hardly audible. "He's..he*'s dead. He was killed in the Boer war."*

"I'm sorry," said the sergeant. *"Is the boy in?"*

"Yes."

"Can we come in?" he asked.

"Yes, it would be better."

The sergeant followed her into the living room which was sparsely furnished but spotlessly clean. The boy, John, was sitting on the settle.

"Johnny this policeman said that you have been playing truant. Is it true?"

The boy, about twelve years of age, looked up at her.

"Yes mam," he murmured.

"Johnny why!" she exclaimed.

The boy shrugged his shoulders and averted his gaze looking down at the floor as though in shame.

"You and another lad broke into the Clarence pottery office and stole five pounds. Didn't you, eh?" demanded the sergeant.

"No sir! I didn't. I never went there." John answered, the

colour of his face turning into a pinkish hue.

"Oh, so where did you go?"

"We went to the moving pictures. The Lyric in Parliament Row".

"And where did you get the money from to get in?" asked the sergeant.

"We sneaked in." Johnny answered quietly.

"Get your jacket on lad and come with me," said the sergeant.

"Where are you taking him?" Mrs. Whalley asked with concern in her voice.

"To the police station. Come on lad, I don't want any fuss."

"But he didn't do it!" exclaimed Mrs. Whalley *"He's told you where he went."*

"He can say what he wants, but we've got a witness. Come on lad."

Electric Theatre, th 'Lyric' Cinema.
Parliament Row, Hanley.

At the magistrates court he was found guilty and sentenced to two years at a Reformatory school. Johnny looked at his mother who sat sobbing in the court.

"I didn't do it mam, I didn't do it!" he cried, and was taken away.

About twelve months into his incarceration, his mother who had been in ill health for some time, exasperated no doubt by the unjust treatment of her only son, died.

A request to the authorities to let John attend his mother's funeral was refused. He was heartbroken, and refused to eat and abide to the harsh regime of the school. He was severely disciplined and force fed. From then on, his character changed he became a rebel against authority and, developed a don't care less attitude, for which he was punished frequently.

On his release, he went to his home, which was by now inhabited by strangers. He was now an orphan, homeless. The only living relative was an uncle who lived in the Neck End of Longton. He was a labourer, and the father of a large family. John had only met the man once, the families not having much to do with one another.

He knocked on the door which was opened by a large unkempt man smelling of beer.

"Wot's they want?" he demanded.

"I'm your nephew John Whalley, I was wondering if you could put me up for a few days?"

"Oh yer did, did yer, well thee cost think agen lad. Ah'll 'ave no thaves in ma ice, so thee cost sod off!"

He was about to slam the door.

"I thought," John quickly said, *"You being my fathers brother..."*

"Thee faither's brother, ah youth? Eh was o'rate till eh met thee stuck up mother, then eh didna want ter know mey. Well ah dunner want ter know they. So sod off!"

The door slammed shut, and John his temper inflamed, infuriated by what the unkempt oaf had said about his mother was about to hammer on the door when he thought better of it and walked away in disgust.

He was now fifteen years of age with no where to live, no job, and sleeping rough he turned to petty crime. stealing food and anything so that he could exist. After a few weeks he eventually was caught and sentenced to two years in a Borstal Institution.
Although the discipline was strict and harsh, he was glad in away, at least he had a roof over his head a bed of sorts to sleep on, and three meals a day.

Horatio Bottomley Campaigning in
Hanley Market Square

He was released when he was seventeen when a mighty war was raging on the continent. It was now 1915 and with the few coppers he had been given on his release he made his way to Hanley. In the Market square a large crowd was assembled, surrounding a dais on which a soldier, a sergeant major was appealing for volunteers.

Behind him a large placard portraying the face of a man wearing officers cap with a large moustache pointing, with a caption, ''YOUR COUNTRY NEEDS YOU.''

He learned later of course, that it was Lord Kitchener, who a year later in 1916, on his way to Russia in H.M.S. Hampshire was mined and he with 800 officers and men were drowned.

He was about to go and find lodgings, when a young man next to him turned to him.

"Do yer want to join?"

Johnny hesitated in his answer, for up to that moment he had considered that he did not owe his country anything, after the way he had been treated so he did not intend to die for it. Now at least for awhile he could take something out of it with board and lodgings and get paid for it.

"Why not" he said, *"lets take the Kings shilling."*

After his medical he was accepted into the army. The harsh discipline of army life held no terrors for him, it was no different than his time in Borstal with one exception which he enjoyed, the freedom when he was allowed out of barracks, and visiting the hostelries in town. This unfortunately was the beginning of his downfall. He acquired a taste for the demon drink, in fact all his meagre army pay was squandered on it.

He was constantly in debt, borrowing from his mates to feed his vice. These halycon days however did not last long, for the reality and horror of warfare was soon thrust upon him, joining the countless thousands of others in the bloodstained battlefields of France. He was a good soldier in the thick of battle, courageous even to the point of foolishness. The battles of the Somme had been conducted on very orthodox military lines. A huge preliminary bombardment of several days gave full indication to the Germans as to where the attack was coming from. They had ample time to prepare. It was thought that the enemy could be shelled out of their position. Only after these battles did military commanders realise that men could endure days of bombardment and survive providing their dugouts were adequately protected. When the British forces advanced against the barbed wire and machine guns that had been well prepared by the German forces, they paid heavily. Altogether 475,000 men were victims of these great battles of the Somme.

Into this blood-letting charged Johnny. Comrades fell on either side of him but he continued to the German lines. An Officer fell severely wounded in front of him, and despite the heavy machine gun fire he struggled to pick up the wounded man on his shoulders and returned him to the British lines. He immediately went back into the fray. For this and other brave deeds he was awarded the Military Medal.

On his leaves he never returned to his native land, because he had no where to stay. He preferred to linger in France enjoying the delights of the small cafe's and the wine. He had a few amorous affairs with the mademoiselles and found places to lay his head.

The war over he returned to Blighty and the town where he was born. There was no welcome home, no trumpet sounding, or cheering crowds for our hero. He felt somehow an outcast.

Staying first in the Salvation Army hostels and lodging houses of the town, drifting from one job to another, losing them all because of drink until he became unemployable. Most of the nights now he languished in a police cell after being picked up by the local gendarmerie for being drunk but not disorderly, he was not a violent man.

On reaching middle age he was a total wreck, and how he existed that long was a mystery. His only apparel except for a pair of old patched and ragged trousers, and a pair of boots which were odd, was his old army great coat. The only income came from shoppers in the town and old soldiers who knew of his bravery in the war. This he spent now on methylated spirits which he obtained from the chemists'. How and where he got food to eat was a mystery.

When the weather was fine he would sleep anywhere if he had got the price of a bed in a lodging house. In winter he was befriended by a pottery kiln fireman who found him a warm corner in which to lay his head.

It was a cold Christmas Eve, the wind bringing squalls of snow that was turning into a blizzard. A solitary figure, head buried in an army great coat collar, reeled drunkenly through the snow singing to himself

"The minstrel boy to the war has gone, in the ranks of dead you will find him."

Passing houses where sounds of merriment came from within. Making his way to the pottery where he would soon find warmth and shelter from this bitter cold.

To his dismay he found that the doors to the pottery were closed. He tried the main gate that also was closed. He had forgotten, due to his almost permanent bemused state, that his friend, the fireman had told him that the oven would not be fired for a few days because of the Christmas holidays. A look of dismay came over his countenance, he took the bottle from his pocket lifted it to his lips and drained the contents.

"I wish you a merry Christmas" he sang, then slithered down the wall of the recess in the gateway.

They found him two days later, buried under the snow, frozen to death, still clutching the bottle.

He that is without sin among you, let him cast the first stone.

NSIO

Type setting and design by
Rose Bank Publishing
Tel: 01785 813633

Printed by Designspeed
Tel: 01782 397796